CW01624556

Brooding Clouds

Phaswane Mpe, 1970–2004.

Brooding Clouds

Phaswane Mpe

UNIVERSITY OF KWAZULU-NATAL PRESS

Published in 2008 by University of KwaZulu-Natal Press
Private Bag X01
Scottsville 3209
South Africa
Email: books@ukznpress.ac.za
Website: www.ukznpress.co.za

ISBN 13: 978-1-86914-101-1

Editor: Elana Bregin
Layout and design: RockBottom Design
Cover design: Flying Ant Designs
Back cover photograph: Glenn Cowley

Printed and bound by Interpak Books, Pietermaritzburg

Contents

Acknowledgements viii
Editor's Preface xi
Epigraph xviii

BROODING CLOUDS

The Open Air 2
Brooding Clouds 3
A Family Story 10
Interlude: Bone Of My Heart 17
Lerato's Ordeal 18
Refentše's Ordeal 24
My Pa Se Kind 31
Occasion For Brooding 32
When I Am Awake 47
Fountains Of Brooding 49
Visions Of A Flying Man 59
Memories Of Silence 62
The Menacing Lights 72
Interlude: Oasis 80
Shades Of Sanctuary 83
Revived Memories 94
Interlude: Memories Of Brooding 104

LOVE, SONGS & BLUES

Sereto Sa Phaswane Mogano 107
Praise Poem Of Phaswane Mogano 108

St Bede's High (Sepedi) 110
St Bede's High (English translation) 111
Moyana Wa Matsikinyane 112
Imagined Walk 113
Marapo A Pelo 114
Little Bee Buzzing 115
Wa Papa 116
Here We Meet Child Of Home 117
In The Depths Of Sleep 119
Mateng-Teng A Boroko 122
X-Mas Love Songs 125
The Picture 127
The Love Beyond 128
Mosong Wola 129
Matsogo 130
Visions Of Joy 132
Dipono Tsa Lethabo 134
Singing The Blues 137
In The Heat Of The Day 138
Time To Rest 140
Nako Ya Maikhutso 142
Our Braamfontein Hobos 144
HIV Nights 146
Elegy For The Trio 147
*love*Life 149
Jude The Obscure 150
The Going 153
Mosepelo 155
Freedom, Love & Songs 157

Dikosa Tsa Tokologo Tsa Lerato 159
Women, Love & Songs, 1956 161
Youth, Love & Songs 163
Half-A-Crown Memory Lane 166
An Ode To Bafana Bafana 168
From Our Hillbrow Tower 172

GOD DOESN'T SMOKE DAGGA

God Doesn't Smoke Dagga 179

Healing With Words: Phaswane Mpe Interviewed
By Lizzy Attree 189

Biographical Note 202
Glossary 204

Acknowledgements

As far as can be ascertained, the following stories and poems have previously appeared in print in the publications stated below. Every effort has been made to credit sources correctly, and any omissions or incorrect details are sincerely regretted. The publishers would welcome updated information in order to amend any errors in the event of a reprint.

Short Stories
'Brooding Clouds' in *imPrint*, 1995; 'Lerato's Ordeal', 'Refentše's Ordeal', 'Occasion For Brooding' and 'Fountains Of Brooding' in *Unity in Flight: Short Fiction* (Botsotso, 2001); 'Brooding Clouds' in *Modern South African Stories* (Ad. Donker, 2002); 'God Doesn't Smoke Dagga' in *Urban '03: Collected New South African Short Stories* (New Africa Books, 2003).

Poetry
'The Open Air' in *New Coin*, 1998; 'Imagined Walk' in *Wits Student*, 1998; 'X-Mas Love Songs' in *English Academy Review*, 1999; 'The Picture' in *Botsotso Magazine*, 2001; 'The Love Beyond' in *English Academy Review*, 1999; 'In The Heat Of The Day' in *Botsotso Magazine*, 2001; 'Time To Rest' in *New Coin*, 1998 and German translation in *Horen*, 2004; 'HIV Nights' in *Words Gone Two Soon*, 2005; 'Elegy For The Trio' in *Nobody Ever Said AIDS: Poems and Stories from Southern Africa*, 2004; in *New Coin*, 2004 and German translation in *Horen*, 2004; 'loveLife' in *Words Gone Two Soon*, 2005 and German translation in *Horen*, 2004; 'Jude The Obscure' in *Blue Fifth Review*, 2003; 'The Going' in *English Academy Review*, 1999; 'An Ode To Bafana Bafana' in *Glass Jars Amongst Trees*, 2003; 'From Our Hillbrow Tower (On Strikes Against Terror)' in *A Generation Defining Itself: In Our Own Words*, 2004 and *Public Culture*, 2004.

Special thanks to Sage Publications, John Thieme of the *Journal of Commonwealth Literature*, and Lizzy Attree for permission to reprint the interview, 'Healing with Words'.

Also to Nape 'a Motana for providing the translations of 'Sereto Sa Phaswane Mogano' and 'St Bede's High', and Vonani Bila for his insights; Meg Samuelson for her helpful input into the collection as a whole; and Wonder Chabalala for his photographic contributions.

Editor's Preface

Brooding Clouds, a collection of short stories and poetry, has been published as a tribute to the creative talent of the late Phaswane Mpe, author of *Welcome To Our Hillbrow* (2001), a debut novel that garnered immediate attention and achieved cult status in South Africa and abroad. The title, *Brooding Clouds*, is taken from the original short story collection written by Phaswane in the 1990s. This constituted, in effect, the prequel manuscript to *Hillbrow*, in which the characters, themes and events of the subsequent novel found their incubation. Although some of these stories have been published individually, the collection in its entirety never found its way into print. This has been an omission long in need of redress, since the short story collection is a work which stands firmly on its own merits.

Imbued with all the charm and ingenuousness of Phaswane's early creativity, the stories evoke the insular rural world of the author's own beginnings, and reflect his emblematic concerns: love, sexual betrayal, poverty, xenophobia, the dislocations of migrancy, and the scourge of 'witch' burning which was of such enduring concern to him. Structured as a series of linked narratives, the stories follow the trials, misfortunes and ambitions of a group of rural youths from the tiny northern village of Tiragalong, as they struggle to escape the 'raving poverty' of their backgrounds and pursue the dream of education that promises redemption. The familiar character cast from *Hillbrow* is here in all its inceptual detail: Tshepo whose calamitous death sets in motion the train of tragic events that unfolds through the rest of the chapters – and on into the pages of *Hillbrow*; Refentše the troubled hero-protagonist; Sammy the betrayer; Lerato 'the Hillbrow woman'; Refilwe, Terror, and others; and, of course, Tiragalong itself, a sometimes sinister puppeteer, jerking the umbilical strings from across the distances, its omniscience fed by the migrant grapevines that travel the highways between Hillbrow/Braamfontein and Tiragalong.

In many respects, the collection constitutes a 1990s period piece. It captures with impeccable insight the nuances of the changing social moment, specifically, the dilemmas of black youths caught between the contexts of rural roots and urban possibility, with their often conflicting survival imperatives and value systems. These were dilemmas with which Phaswane himself was very familiar.

The title story, 'Brooding Clouds', together with its companion pieces, 'Occasion For Brooding' and 'Fountains Of Brooding', offers strong commentary on the village obsessions with 'night prowlers' and their arts, setting up a black comedy of errors that is a harsh indictment of the superstitious absurdity of witch-burning, and its self-styled proponents who seek to 'cleanse' the village of misfortune by making scapegoats of the old. Other pieces, such as 'Lerato's Ordeal' and 'Refentše's Ordeal' provide some of the background detail on the circumstances that lead to the *Hillbrow* lovers finally taking the plunge and revealing their feelings for each other. The final story, 'Memories Of Brooding', infuses a welcome closing note of optimism, invoking the hope that resides in Tiragalong's younger generation, with their easier access to affluence and assertive confidence that makes them less susceptible to Tiragalong's thrall.

Interfused with the stories are several poetic interludes that add their more complex dimension to the narratives. Some of these poems were written as part of the original collection – much of it penned, interestingly, during Phaswane's sojourn in Oxford in 1997 – while others were included later because he felt they slotted in so well with the story themes.

Phaswane was a writer totally rooted in the context of his personal and geographical worlds. Hillbrow and Tiragalong, the twin nodes of his psyche, were not just place to him, but identity, woven into the experiential fabric of his being. It was this strong and intimate bond with his environment that gave the power to his pen. The storylines and characters in *Brooding Clouds* clearly have a lot of Phaswane's own experiences in them, and in this sense stand as a testimony to his life as much as his literary talent.

Like his characters, he too battled to escape the crushing early poverty that often cuts short the potential of youths like Tshepo; like Refentše, he felt keenly the alienating aspects of undergraduate university life, with its lack of tangible support for those carrying the weight of their disadvantaged backgrounds, hamstrung as they were by the twin legacies of poverty and Bantu Education. He knew what it was to 'survive on lice', while struggling under the crippling financial burdens of student loans; and he felt the acute pressure not to fail, not just on his own account, but inflated by the hope invested in him by family and community.

His own life was dogged by 'brooding clouds' – a metaphor which became the allegory for so much in his writing. It evokes the thirsty land of physical and psychic drought where clouds gather but never release into rain; the sinister subtext of violence that runs through the narratives and dogs the footsteps of his characters; and the depressive emotional states that hover like engulfing miasma over the afflicted ones. But most of all, the image conjured up for him the overhanging balconies of Hillbrow highrises that loom overhead with menacing portent as one looks up from below them.

It is interesting that so much of Phaswane's creative output – the major portion of the *Brooding Clouds* stories, most of the poems, and the *Hillbrow* novel – seems to have emerged within a relatively short timespan, between 1997 and 2000. This fact is perhaps what gives his work its prismatic effect. Poems, stories and novel seem not to follow one another in linear sequence, so much as erupt together – tangential strands of the complex Phaswane mind. His writing has the spatial configuration of a musical score, with all the different segments sounding forth simultaneously, each resonating – and reflecting – off the others, adding new facets to the whole.

This is nowhere more evident than in his poetry, which makes up the second part of this compilation. Titled *Love, Songs & Blues*, the collection comprises 37 English and Sepedi poems, most of the latter being the author's adaptations of his English originals. Only two of the Sepedi poems, 'Sereto Sa Phaswane Mogano' – 'Praise Poem Of

Phaswane Mogano' – and 'St Bede's High', were originally composed in that language, and for the purposes of this collection have been translated in slightly adapted form – their complexity defies any literal attempt – by Sepedi author, Nape 'a Motana. The decision to showcase the Sepedi poems in the main body of the collection, rather than placing them into a separate section, has been taken in consideration of Phaswane's love for his home tongue. Sepedi was so much a matter of the heart to him. His great wish was to have the language recognised on its own merits, and he frequently lamented the lack of opportunities for publishing Sepedi works. He had begun the major undertaking of adapting his *Love, Songs & Blues* poems into Sepedi and had previously translated the entire *Brooding Clouds* collection, under the title of *Maru a Maso*. This remains, to date, unpublished.

It should be mentioned that the stories and poems in this collection have been presented as far as possible true to their original form and order. There has been a conscious attempt to keep editorial input to a minimum, preserving the material intact as Phaswane first penned it in order to let through his inimitable voice and thought processes. We encounter here the expressive quirks and little stylistic tricks that were so much his trademark: the individualistic syntax and circuitous sentence construction, the recurring stock phrases and fondness for double negatives; the circular and layered story development that unfolds in tangential strands, with the same events retold from different points of view, each yielding up new pieces of the puzzle; and the penchant for mixed metaphor that reflected Phaswane's love of language and his deep affinity with words: 'A glitter of disappointment showed its face to his heart'; 'A tentative shimmer of hope, emerging during the period of waiting, struggled in the iron grip of giant pessimism in his chest'. Who but Phaswane could conjure up such imagery and get away with it?

He was the master of stream of consciousness writing, seen to such good effect in *Hillbrow*, and in his *Love, Songs & Blues* poems. Some of the poems, with their powerful narrative currents, exert an almost centrifugal force, sweeping the reader up in unpunctuated streams and whirling loops of imagery, to arrive, breathless, at the core.

It is in his poetry that Phaswane exposes most deeply the passion, idealism and conscience that were his, pouring himself without reservation into the people and places he loved, and which were so much a part of his being and identity: Hillbrow; the xenophobia of Hillbrow; Braamfontein hobos; painful loves, sexual betrayals, degradation, despair; the Quartz Street pavement brothels, and the migrants who avail themselves there with thoughtless irresponsibility; the non-accountable acts of procreation that spawn life and abandon it, without regard for the human detritus that results; the careless hedonism of student life; HIV/AIDS; global conflict. These topicalities are brought vividly to life by the poet's observant and compassionate eye. It is perhaps the more recent, undated, poems in *Love, Songs & Blues*, probably composed between 2002 and 2003, that reveal most strongly the progression of his skill, and the mastery and confidence that came to hone his earlier style.

Completing this collection is 'God Doesn't Smoke Dagga' – the last short story to be written by Phaswane, in March 2003. Originally commissioned by New Africa Books for its *Urban '03* anthology, it is a moody and powerful piece that makes a fitting coda to this compilation. It emerged out of a long creative drought, a writer's block induced in part by the bouts of chronic ill health Phaswane battled towards the end of his life. But when it did appear, it gushed forth in characteristic form: Phaswane completed it in one sitting, typing away non-stop all night until late the following afternoon. Strong, moving and highly original in its conception, it shows the maturation of Phaswane's eclectic style, weaving together the strands of personal pain and inner-city context that was his speciality. The title in itself is irresistably Phaswane, and the writing has been honed here to a cryptic art of understatement that challenges the reader's perceptual frame with its allusive – and elusive – unfolding.

Finally, we are pleased to be able to include one of the last interviews conducted with Phaswane, by Lizzy Attree, just before his death in 2004. Titled 'Healing With Words', it allows Phaswane's voice a final say, and gives the opportunity for him to speak for himself on a range of topics and issues.

Phaswane's premature death has been a great loss to literature in South Africa, not just because of his stature as a writer, but on account of the singular human being that he was. The range of works presented here underscores the clear trajectory of his creative star, his growth as an author and poet, and the steady expansion in his vision and literary grasp, which held the promise of even more dazzling fruition in the future. There is some comfort in knowing that his presence lives on vividly through his writing, and in the 'afterlife' of memory of those who knew and love him. It is easy to imagine that, like Refentše in *Welcome To Our Hillbrow*, Phaswane is looking down from 'the lounge of Heaven', and applauding the publication of this lifework collection.

Elana Bregin
Durban, December 2007

Note

For ease of reference a selected Glossary of mainly South African terms has been included on p. 204. In certain instances, where the meaning of words is crucial to the understanding of a poem, explanatory footnotes have been provided.

'Nothing much happens at the very end – just a bird perching on a wicket in the greyness of a wet day.'
(Vladimir Nabokov, Glory*)*

Brooding Clouds

The Open Air

i watch
scattered clouds gather
around the hot ember
that tours those blue heavens
the cracked clay of tiragalong
whimpers el nino el nino
brooding clouds cast merciless glances
at the pleading eyes
& floods throw chunks of soil
into a vomiting river
& torrents of woes
drown the open air of the countryside
while livestock shocked
by their bony brethren
reflected in the shattered mirrors
deep down those oceans of clay
where water could have been
moo and bleat
green peace
now . . .

Brooding Clouds

It is the beginning of autumn, the season in which the people of Tiragalong, a tiny village not far from Pietersburg, tend to look younger because of the nourishment they get from their abundant harvest. It is autumn, but this year the fields show no signs of life. Mealie plants are grey – grey like ash. Trees have lost their leaves, which turned sickly yellow before their time. Grass is dry already, and there have been several veld fires. The nearest river is so dry, livestock go there only to look at the cracked clay where water used to be. Even the word 'livestock' is misleading, for here are merely collections of bones in the shapes of cattle, sheep and goats.

Everything is dry. One does not need the help of a sangoma to predict that, towards the end of the season, when harvest time knocks on the doors of the villagers, there shall be nothing to reap. The rains take some pleasure in not relieving this tiny village. The old men, sitting under the trees whose shades are no match for the scorching sun, complain that the Gods have turned their backs on them.

Makgolo is one of the oldest women in the village. Tonight she is alone in her hut. She sits with her legs stretched out before her. Her eyes stare vacantly at the fireplace. The fire has been out for quite a long time but Makgolo does not notice. She rubs her hands together like a person who is just warming them up a bit.

Tonight she has no children to tell stories to. A dreadful thing happened yesterday. Although children love her stories – she tells the most beautiful stories in the village and its neighbourhood – they shall not come to listen to her any more.

Her stories begin, almost always, like this: 'Long, long ago, when stones were still soft and edible and trees could walk . . . ' Who does not want to know what happened in those good old days? Children are fascinated by her stories, stories of witchcraft and ordinary lives, of poverty and abundance, of wars and peace. The children give very little heed to the moral side of her tales.

But Makgolo has no audience tonight. She whiles the time away by drawing patterns in the air with her failing eyes. The thickening darkness in the hut sharpens the bright edges of her mental pictures. She is the solitary watcher of her own art. She has to be alone. Has not the boy Thušo come running in the heat of the afternoon sun to warn her to fly away on her broom? He overheard a group of youngsters who called themselves Comrades talk about Makgolo.

'She is a witch,' they said, 'and can fly on a broom. What is more, she has sent lightning to strike Tshepo.'

Tshepo was a young man of promise, coming from a poor family. His father was killed in Alexandra for reasons unknown to his family and the village. His mother did not even own a fowl. The mother and son lived on lice, as the villagers would say. But her brother who, although not really wealthy, was far better off than herself, assisted in the education of her only son.

For his part, Tshepo did a lot. His mother had said to him when he went off to commence his studies at a university: 'Son, our elders might have been defeated by whites. But they were not utterly stupid. They always said to us, "Bask in the sun when it still shines. Tomorrow it may shine on others and leave you in the cold." So, my child, go to the university; and do your work when you get there. The sun shines. Go bask in it. Think about your mother at home. And show some gratitude to your uncle.'

Tshepo kept these words in his heart. His mother was not the sort of person who gave sermons. When she did, it was with utmost love and warmth. After her words, Tshepo felt warm liquid flood his eyes. He turned around quickly to hide the tears, for he was not circumcised for nothing. He had not cried when that old man cut the foreskin from his penis with agonising slowness.

He liked to relive the experience in his memory. It was worth reliving. After all, he did not cry! Not many boys could boast that. But there he was now, his tears betraying him before a woman.

His mother saw them. She came nearer, embraced him tenderly, and kissed them dry.

At the university Tshepo worked hard. Although he failed to complete the requirements for his degree in record time, he managed to get it with an upper second-class pass. It was on the day he received his sparkling results that the fatal lightning struck him. There was nothing one could really call rain. Just black clouds, brooding for a long time over the village. The people, seeing such ugly clouds, feared a devilish storm after the drought that had done enough damage already. Blinding lightning tore the black clouds mercilessly, and rumbling thunder backed it up. But rain, no! Only a few drops that left the land as dry as a bleached bone. The clouds dragged their feet away when the blowing horn mournfully announced Tshepo's death.

On receiving the message concerning the calamity that had befallen her son, Tshepo's mother choked with grief. Thus, mother and son took leave of the village of Tiragalong in order that they might go to live in the underworld.

Makgolo had not always been an outcast. She was once a respected member of society. Things changed quite late in her life, with the death of her husband. The husband, after years and years of having deserted Makgolo, suddenly returned home.

All the years he had been away, Makgolo had had to fend for herself without an assistant. She fared quite well. She was not one of those people who simply sat on their hands. She put her hands, and all her physical strength, to tilling the land and producing enough food for herself. Even children who came to hear her stories were offered a mealie, a melon, and other products of her labour. The other reason she was able to cope was simply that she had no children of her own. When the husband left her for good – until his fateful return, that is – she was without a child.

During the time that the husband was gone Makgolo, in fending for herself, secured a more caring man. This man, Kereng, in addition to looking after his large family, did whatever manly deed was necessary in Makgolo's compound. And people did not see this as bad, nor did they begrudge Makgolo his help.

'How could she do without the likes of him?' they said. 'Her own man was surely irresponsible, or else how could he desert such a wife as Makgolo?'

The problem, really, was the husband's return. He looked healthy enough on his arrival. However, within a few days of his return he developed a strange illness. Makgolo, bitter that he imposed himself upon her as head of the family he cared little to build, and regretting that those worthy of such titles were denied them, refused to take the man to a herbalist. It was too costly, she said unashamedly, to take a man there, more especially a man who had deserted her for that long. Staying by himself for all that time – it was rumoured that he worked in the mines in the South – the husband must surely have saved up a little, and could therefore take care of himself.

So he was left to die within two weeks of his return. Thus, a solid ground for rumours was laid.

Gossip, to the effect that Makgolo had bewitched him, began to do the rounds in Tiragalong. She did not want to lose Kereng, they said. So, naturally, her own husband had to be removed from the face of the earth. Others said that it must have been Kereng who had killed the husband, because he was not prepared to lose Makgolo, who was obviously a much better partner than his own wife. Yet others said that if, indeed, it was Kereng, then it was because Makgolo had spiced his food with I-am-the-only-one, a love potion that makes you love a person so much that you would be prepared to destroy whoever happens to come between you and the loved one. Because men were not generally known for dealing in witchcraft, it was, in the end, obvious that Makgolo had done it.

When Kereng mysteriously died from a similar disease, the truth finally revealed itself. For who has ever heard of a witch, or a wizard for that matter, who bewitched themselves?

Hard times followed for mothers, who were at pains to stop their children from visiting the witch. But parents were parents; their interests were not one with the interests of their children. These children could not be told the full story about Makgolo. They repeatedly failed to understand their parents' desire to deny them the chance to listen to Makgolo's stories, and to benefit from her open-handedness.

Children went on visiting her. As nothing frightening happened in the village after Kereng's death, their daily rounds to her hut were not disrupted seriously.

With Tshepo's death, the youth felt that Makgolo was having it too much her own way. Her childlessness was no excuse for causing her neighbour to become childless like her. Tshepo's mother was too good a woman to deserve this harsh treatment. It was high time that she had a rest while her son provided for her. Besides, where was the village going to get another fine chap like him from?

Tshepo had made a name for the village by going to study in the South. He was then intending to teach at the local school. No! Children could not be deprived of a proper education simply because of the jealousy of this old witch!

The youth of Tiragalong called a meeting. In that meeting they decided that the village should be cleansed. The youth were not going to sit back and simply watch while their efforts to bring progress to the village were threatened.

'But let us seek direction first,' one Comrade suggested. 'Do we really want to necklace wrong people unwittingly?'

Most of the Comrades agreed that this was a wise suggestion. Representatives were accordingly sent to consult bone throwers in some of the distant villages, in which they might find truly great practitioners of the bone-throwing art. But first, money was collected from every homestead in Tiragalong. Bone throwers, like everyone else, had families to feed. On their return, the representatives gave their report. Indeed, Tshepo had been bewitched by an old woman to the east of his homestead, they said. The descriptions of this woman could only point to Makgolo, they said.

The few who could have spoken up for Makgolo, who saw nothing to prove that she was a witch, were afraid to do so. The thought that they might be said to support her because they were receiving lessons in witchcraft from her, was enough to pull them back from defending her. Such an accusation would have meant that whatever step would be taken against witchcraft and its practitioners would also be taken against them.

Makgolo sits alone in her hut. Her eyes are lifted to the roof of the hut. Through the tiny holes in the thatch she can catch faint glimpses of the evening sky. Or maybe faint stars, since it is too dark for her to see the sky. The roof itself, and indeed the stars as well, would have been invisible in the darkness. Only, she looks at them through her mind. The thatch is so dry it has turned white like her hoary hair. Thatch burns easily. If those Comrades should come . . .

Oh, their song is audible already! Fear seizes her. The freedom songs become louder. The Comrades are approaching fast. Makgolo's fear grows with the loudness of the songs.

'They say I am a witch . . . ' Her mind is engrossed with these words. And she imagines that the songs are about witchcraft.

'They say I am a witch . . . '

Makgolo does not understand the songs. She cannot understand them, for they are sung in isiZulu. If she knew isiZulu she would realise that the language of the songs is bad isiZulu. The Comrades are singing political songs, songs that freedom fighters used to sing in the apartheid era, willing new, hopefully democratic, governance into being. The Comrades sing in bad isiZulu because they, too, are strangers to the language. But they do not think much about the un-Zuluness of their freedom songs. What matters is that they should cleanse their village. They shall sweep into the roaring flames of their rage all the scorpions in the village. Witchcraft shall be no more!

'They say I am a witch . . . '

Makgolo's thatched hut catches the fire of her own imagination. Her screams are not of the imagination, though. Her screams confirm to the Comrades that she is already being haunted by bloody conscience. Before they can even touch her.

Witchcraft shall be no more!

The police will soon come to investigate, as usual. The Comrades will have already fled their village for fear of Mankweng police, who are known for kicking a tsotsi until it does mischief in its pants. Two of the Comrades are on their way to a neighbouring village. They, too, have fled their home village.

'You know, I wanted to cry 'Stop!' to the crowd. I simply could not stand the smell . . . ' The first Comrade – 'Professor', as he was nicknamed – breaks the silence.

His companion, Sammy, agrees that the smell of the burning necklaces and petrol was undoubtedly extremely offensive.

'Absolutely. But it is neither the tyres nor the petrol I meant. I was talking about the smell of her roasting flesh . . . '

Sammy tries to stop Professor from talking. He would rather not hear more. But the other is not to be silenced.

'Was she really a witch? Did she send lightning to strike Tshepo?'

'Who knows?' is all Sammy can offer.

Professor heaves a big sigh. There follows another profound silence.

A Family Story

Mogau shocked Tiragalong when he decided that he would join the police force. Mankweng Police, or any other police, were not popular in the village. It was not just that they arrested the Comrades every time the latter cleansed their village by necklacing to death all the practitioners of witchcraft in Tiragalong. What the Comrades hated most about the police was the cruelty with which they treated the Comrades at the police station.

That anyone from the Comrade circles should enlist was in itself a betrayal. But what was really shocking was that it was Mogau. For the village had persuaded itself that Mogau would become a professor. His teachers talked about his school work with reverence. They always emphasised how bright he was, and how he was obviously not born by accident – he came here to do important things in life. It was one of his classmates, Tsakane, a child of Nobody, with her repertoire of English vocabulary, that nicknamed him Professor.

Many villagers did not quite know what 'Professor' meant. They were glad to learn that it was another word for a university teacher. It was clear to them that that was one of the highest professions. None of the villagers had held such a position before. Tshepo was going to be the first villager, except for the school principal, to get a degree, had it not been for the lightning. For some time the village had hoped that at least one of its children would follow in Tshepo's footsteps. For the neighbouring villages were doing well, and outstripping Tiragalong by far in that regard.

Most of Tiragalong's youths chose to read for teachers' diplomas in the colleges of Lebowa. There were a few who studied at the University of the North, which was the nearest university to the village. But, in general, the teachers at Tiragalong High seemed to have accepted that teaching diplomas were what most of their students should be aiming for. They seldom spoke highly of such students.

But Professor's group was exceptional; the teachers remarked on that when the group was still doing its Standard Eight. And it had maintained its reputation for hard work and intellectual ability right up until it went for its Standard Ten. Of this exceptional group, Professor was the person to bet on most highly.

Throughout their matric year, the teachers had urged Professor and other promising classmates, such as Sammy, Refentše and Tsakane, to consider applying to the University of Witwatersrand in Johannesburg. They constantly reminded the group of Tshepo's impressive performance in that tough environment and how he had made a name for the school. Surely, the teachers urged, Professor and his classmates could accept the challenge of taking Tshepo's achievements further?

And so Professor and the others had applied for admission to the university in Johannesburg. They were granted provisional admission without a problem, while they waited for their final exam results. The teachers were overjoyed. Here at last, they boasted to teachers from other schools, were some of their products who bore testimony to the fact that some teaching had been done at Tiragalong High. They talked about these products as if they were already enrolled at the university.

For Professor, it was a problem that first tentatively peeped with sinister grin from round a corner when he announced to his parents that he intended to go to Jo'burg for his degree studies. His father asked him if that would not incite the jealousy of their relatives, from whom they had had to flee when Professor was only two years old.

This was news to Professor. He knew that his parents had lived in Nobody, about twenty-five kilometres north of Pietersburg, before they came to Tiragalong. What he was not told, and which came out at this awkward moment, was that their resolution to leave Nobody was forced on them.

According to his father, Professor was their third born. His two sisters died only a few months after their births. He himself nearly died at the age of two. The issue was fairly complex, the father said. For his mother's family had not wanted their daughter to be married to a poor man. The father's family also objected to the marriage, on grounds that his mother's family had mastered the art of witchcraft. They said that her family must also have taught it to their daughter. Or that she had learnt the art of flying on a broom at night by herself. A baby snake is born a snake, the father was reminded. They were not going to rear snakes in the family. So Professor's parents had offended their families and relatives by insisting on the marriage.

They were not aware that the offence was very serious until Professor got ill and it looked as if he would bid them farewell like his sisters. They consulted the greatest doctor in Tzaneen. The main attraction about him was that, as a distant outsider, he would not know them. Whatever he had to tell them would not be based on personal jealousies and grudges. He was thus more likely than most to give an unbiased diagnosis of their child's illness. Or so they thought.

When they set eyes on the doctor, Mogau's father seemed, vaguely, to recall having seen his face somewhere. Perhaps at Nobody, or in one of the neighbouring villages. The father was not unduly disturbed by this, however. For doctors who do not travel could only starve their families. What did not occur to the father was that, like others of his ilk, this bone thrower was an inquisitive specimen, one who asked questions and made it his business to know people and their lineages wherever he went. As Mogau's parents greeted him and introduced each other, he would be making important links in his head.

After consulting his bones, the bone thrower had looked gloomily at them. The boy could die at any time, he said in a melancholy tone. He went into the history of their marriage. He talked at length about how one paternal aunt, in particular, took it as a personal affront when the parents married without her blessings. It was she who was causing them all this grief. When the first child caught what they had taken to be measles, she was in fact possessed of an evil spirit inspired into her heart by the aunt. The same went for the second child, who died of bad tonsils, or so everyone thought.

'As long as you remain close to your sister,' the doctor had suggested, looking at Mogau's father with a protracted stare, 'your children will continue to be vivid reminders of your contempt for her.'

Both Professor's parents had had nothing but love for this aunt. They found it strange that she could interpret their innocent family matters as signs of contempt.

Professor's father was particularly grieved. It had never occurred to him that his sister could be a witch. Since she was not married, no other family could be blamed for teaching her the art. It was a weird thought that she could have learnt it from his own family. Surely it could not be from his own mother? She used to criticise witchcraft so much and was openly outspoken against it.

But then, so was the sister . . . What did it all mean? He then remembered the saying in Tiragalong, that witches had no skin colour that differentiated them from the rest of the society.

It was the doctor who suggested that two or more opinions were always better than one.

'Even the Gods get it wrong sometimes,' he said. He recommended that they visit another doctor in the neighbouring village.

'If you visited him straight away, you could be sure that I had not spoken to him yet,' the doctor concluded, putting the bones back into their animal-skin bag.

They thanked him for this advice. On the way home, they praised the bone thrower's modesty. It was customary for these doctors to pretend to have so much confidence in their bones that they would go so far as to declare that they would throw them away, and risk the wrath of their Ancestors, should the bones tell anything but the truth.

As it was, Professor's parents did not visit the second doctor. What was the point? Had the first bone thrower not told them a mouthful already? It was clear to Professor's parents that their family was not safe with the father's parents and sisters around them. Of the two, the mother had the more worrying opinion. She said that even when all her children had died, her husband's sisters would still not be satisfied.

'No matter how many cattle you put in their hearts' kraals,' she said, 'the kraals will never get full. You are their brother. They will not harm you. All I am saying is that I am not their sister. That is all.' As she said these words, she was trying hard to hold back tears of disappointment with her in-laws.

Professor's father felt chilly drops of sweat form on his back and slowly trickle down at the thought of losing his wife. It was more than enough that they had already lost two children. Thinking about his parents and siblings, he was tempted to doubt the doctor's words. But again he remembered that witchcraft is colourless. He could not take further risks by letting blood ties shatter his family. He looked at the agonised face of the bone of his heart. Yes, she was right, he concluded. They had to leave blood ties behind.

So they left Nobody for Tiragalong. Tiragalong was fairly new-founded then. It was, and remains, the tiniest of the villages in that part of the world, even with its steady growth.

Their move to Tiragalong did not enable Professor's parents to talk openly about the forces behind their departure from Nobody. They feared that whirlwinds might blow their words as far as Nobody. And perhaps risk offending their pursuers even more.

As for Professor, he was at that stage too young to be told this troubling story. Definitely too young, in the parents' eyes, to be trusted to shield it from the reach of ever-prying eyes and open ears, always ready to pounce on and devour any latest piece of gossip they could get their claws and teeth into. The parents had to save their child. Even if that meant keeping their oppressive silence for years.

Professor was shaken by the story. When his results came, they provided an occasion for brooding. He was the only one from Tiragalong High to pass Standard Ten with distinction. On the day the results arrived, the principal announced proudly to everyone who set foot on the school premises that the distinction was one of only five in the whole of Mankweng Circuit.

'The whole of Mankweng Circuit!' he rolled the words again and again around his tongue, savouring the beauty of their taste.

His parents, Professor knew, would be happy that he had distinguished himself. But it would be a haunted happiness. For, with their strong convictions, they would only see in his success the danger of the aunt's attention being drawn relentlessly towards the object of her gross jealousy.

Professor himself had a different opinion of the aunt. He thought she was very loving. Whenever she visited them, she had brought something for him – books were her favourite presents to her nephew. Professor found it impossible to confess to his parents that it was partly through her constant encouragement that he earned such a reputation for himself and his school in the whole of Mankweng Circuit.

Professor was aware that he was not his parents. He knew that they would only have seen his aunt's overtures as the fattening of the bull before the day of its slaughter arrived. They had watched his aunt with their hearts sinking into the abyss of fear and the grey matter between their ears straining to work out ways of pulling her back from their son without showing her that they saw through her cunning. The aunt had kept on visiting. And, as Professor now knew, the parents had continued to sigh endlessly, sighs of powerlessness and despair at their inability to tell her what they already knew about her hidden snares.

It was on the very day Professor received his own results that Tshepo got struck by lightning. Tiragalong felt the blow strongly because Tshepo's mother, who was respected in the village, soon followed her son as a result of grief.

'See,' Professor's father pointed out to him, 'there are witches all over. It can only be jealousy that has led to the bright boy's death. Or else why would the lightning have waited until he received his results? You don't know how you worry us, child, with your ambition.'

The father shook his head gently but meaningfully.

So Professor, for fear of making his parents live in fear while he studied in Jo'burg, resolved that he would abandon his plans and instead quietly study by correspondence with the University of South Africa. He would not even tell his parents of these intentions, he decided. In the meantime, he must be seen to be doing something towards shaping his future. He would make sure to avoid anything glamorous. Anything which could be related, even remotely, to education.

He enlisted to be trained as a police officer at Mankweng. At least the nine months of training and the subsequent appointment would be for free. With the money thus earned as a police officer, he would be able to pay his study fees. This would ensure that he didn't have to tell his parents about his studies, as he would not need their money. His correspondence with the university could always be directed to his place of work. It was going to be that simple.

Professor knew from the beginning that the Comrades would be disappointed in him. He also knew that he would have to decide between satisfying them, and in that way keep his parents unhappy, or evade his parents' unhappiness by risking the wrath of the Comrades. He put the two choices in his hands to weigh.

At least the Comrades would not kill him, he decided. They only killed witches. All they could do was to treat him like an outcast. He could live with that. Not altogether happily, but he could live with it all right. And when he had earned enough money later in life, he could relocate to Jo'burg, or to any other place that he chose, where he would not be too much in the Comrades' faces. The laws that prevented people from living in the posh suburbs of the city had been scrapped. He could see his way out of the dark caves of witchcraft and Comradeship, witch hunting and subsequent necklacings. It was not an easy path to walk. But it was there for him to travel, if he dared.

What appeared to him to be the more daunting choice was the prospect of grieving his parents for a number of years by going off to study in Jo'burg. He knew well that grief could be as fatal as lightning. The story of Tshepo and his mother's resulting death was still fresh in Tiragalong's mind. Professor found the thought of burying his parents, whom he himself would, in effect, have killed, unappealing. He was going to try his best to keep them satisfied.

But he was shortly to realise that he did not know his parents half as well as he had thought. For when he told his father of his new intentions, the latter was not pleased. He was, in fact, quite disappointed that his son, who had done so much better than any other youth in his class, and in the whole of Mankweng Circuit, should choose to follow one of the least respected directions in life.

Interlude: Bone Of My Heart

the ember
rises above the eastern mountains
throws its bright sparks toward the corners
of the earth
you catch a few & pile them
onto the dry twigs at the hearth
of your heart
with gentle breeze blowing inward
they rub against the dryness
& like a timid child summoned
a flame emerges
the heart warms up to the approaching innocence of the child
& with slow gentle lips you impart
some of the morning joy onto mine
the bone of my heart

Lerato's Ordeal

It was not very bright in the bar. The main lights were switched off. The only lighting issued forth from the TV screen. Lerato and two fellow students sat close to the TV set. Jack stood behind the counter, from where he was selling the beer and watching the TV as well. They were all arguing about who the player of the day was in the rugby match.

Refentše walked in, greeted them with his usual cheerfulness. Lerato did not need to catch the whiffs of lager from his breath to realise that he was a little excited. Excited, for he had always refused to call himself drunk. The two exchanged a few pleasantries. Refentše then approached Jack. Lerato's eyes wandered back to the TV screen, while her ears were divided between the TV sound and Refentše's voice, the voice of the secret bone of her heart.

'Two cases of cans, please,' Refentše said. Jack asked what the occasion was.

'We have won, brother! That's it! Those New Zealanders thought that they owned this game of rugby. We have won!'

Lerato smiled to herself as Refentše praised the Springboks for winning the Rugby World Cup. She knew Refentše did not care much about sport, especially rugby. His praise could only be a joke, made even lighter by its feebleness as a justification for swallowing so much lager.

Lerato knew that Refentše would have come to buy large quantities of beer, regardless. In the early days when they first got to know each other, in her first year of studies at the university, Lerato used to wonder when Refentše did his readings, with so much drinking going on. She discovered that he usually bought his beer and drank it while reading. Unlike most students that she knew who indulged in taking these waters, Refentše had never yet submitted a late essay.

'Time management!' he had told her once, when she suggested that perhaps books and drink did not go together.

She was aware that Refentše bought the beer now, if for no other reason, then at least to keep him company while he worked on the assignment due soon. Rugby could be no strong reason for deterring him from his work.

As Refentše turned around to leave, he found himself facing the mouth of a gun, behind which was a balaclava, so that he could not see the face.

'Face down!'

Jack, Lerato and the other two students in the bar threw themselves down immediately. Refentše remained standing. Lerato's heart missed many beats. She wanted to shout, 'Refentše!'

'Come out from behind the counter!' Instructions hissed from the balaclava.

And to Refentše: 'Face down!'

The balaclava was slowly approaching him. As this second order hissed out from between the lips of the balaclava, another balaclava appeared at the slightly open door. It shifted over somewhat to allow a third one to appear, also pointing a gun at whoever might be in the bar. This third invader retreated as soon as he had appeared, and gently closed the door behind him.

The first invader was still approaching Refentše. Lerato could see the dim shape of the gun pointing at her best university friend, who could have become her lover had he initiated the discussion to that effect. Lerato had for a long time been wishing that he would, sooner rather than later. The gunman came closer. Lerato's fear created visions of her friend's stubbornness taking him into the grave. She heard voices singing the familiar funeral song, 'We are just passers-by on this earth'.

Refentše had often talked to her about the importance of being stubborn. He first raised this issue when she was intimidated in class by their lecturer. She had thought of de-registering because of it. She meant to spend the rest of the following term at home, thinking deeply about whether she really wanted to have a degree, if getting one meant cruel exposures to lecturers' whims. She would have left the university at that point had Refentše not talked to her about respecting herself, and not letting anyone trample her down.

After a lengthy talk, in which he cited many examples of people who were nearly destroyed – and some who were indeed destroyed – by careless comments from their seniors, Refentše concluded: 'If you leave, you can be sure that Dr Lewi's opinion that you are not university material will be vindicated.'

He had given her a mission to prove to herself that she was worth more than Dr Lewi reckoned.

But, as she lay there now on the carpeted floor, she could not persuade herself that stubbornness should be pushed to the very limits the way Refentše was doing. She raised her head a little, thought about standing up and going over to pull Refentše down onto the floor. But then she thought about what might be going on in the mind of the balaclava man. Pictures of her miserable friend who had been raped in an ordeal involving car robbery cut across her mind with sharp strokes. They mingled uneasily with visions of Refentše's corpse and the mournful tones of 'We are just passers-by on this earth'.

So she remained glued to the carpet, with fright stifling her attempt to call out to Refentše to do what they were all doing.

The man in the balaclava approached nearer still.

'Don't try my patience . . . I said, "Face down!"'

The icy tone of the voice sent a chilly tremor down Lerato's back. She could feel cold sweat trickling down the valley between her breasts.

Refentše seemed to have come back to his senses. Not as quickly as Lerato would have wished. Unlike Jack, Refentše did not hurl himself onto the cold tiles immediately. He walked towards the carpeted area, where Lerato and the others were lying. Lerato's visions of Refentše's corpse, of the men in balaclavas bumping off her friend, were becoming sharper by the second.

With startling bends of the imagination she would then substitute herself for the gang-raped friend . . .

'Where is Jack?'

'Here.' Jack's voice was faint.

Lerato's thought patterns followed the aggressive questions and the timid replies. She could not decide what Jack might have done to deserve death by shooting. It was not just that he was a good soul; no, it was more than that . . . but anyway, she loved Refentše far more . . . much too much to be able to keep her attention on Jack for very long. Lerato told herself that Jack would be the first victim, and hence lucky enough not to have to experience the mounting pain of waiting for his death while watching others go before him. Then it would be Refentše's turn . . . or the two students lying on either side of her on the carpet . . .

'Where are the car keys?'

'Here.' Again, faintly.

'Throw them in front of you!'

Jack used the university car occasionally, on weekends, to carry beer from the brewery to the Parktown Village bar. On these occasions, he would also take advantage of the car to visit his girlfriend and, often, bring her along to the Village. For her sake, Lerato was thankful that she was not there with them this time. But she could not dwell on this streak of thought for more than half a second.

Jack threw the keys down in front of him, towards the invader. The second invader picked them up. Apparently having decided that the students were entirely harmless, the second invader said to his companion, 'Keep order!' and went out.

The first invader stayed behind.

Jack moved slightly, in order to make himself more comfortable. The gun pointed in his direction instantly.

Lerato shut her eyes quickly . . . she opened them just as quickly. She coughed – a stifled kind of cough that, she hoped, would not irritate the gunman. She could not force herself to forget that she was the only woman in there. She saw herself melting into pictures in the following day's newspaper and TV headlines. She listened to the haunting echoes, as if originating from within her own skull, of voices in the streets, singing 'Amabokoboko aya phumelela . . . '

Presently, the gun pointed at Refentše. Again Lerato shut her eyes quickly, with a pang she had never imagined she could experience in her life. She had always liked Refentše. Now, his impending death forced her into severe self-reproach. She had let cowardice reign in her heart. She would have told Refentše how much she loved him, had she not overwhelmed herself with the thought that, when they got to know that she was the one who had initiated their potential love life, people would say that she was a whore. Now, in the fragmented, tormenting review of her own life and her relationship with Refentše, as she lay there on the carpet, she wondered if whoredom did not reside in the failure to pour unreservedly the deep passions of her heart into her beloved's ears and heart.

'Switch that shit off!' The gun pointed itself at the TV set this time.

Refentše stood up, slowly. The slowness of his movements made his death a certainty in Lerato's mind. He was sure to be the first victim . . .

He switched it off. Guided in the dimness from the lights outside the bar, he went back to his former place.

'Not there, cheeky bastard! Come over here.'

He stood up. He went down again, right at the feet of his tormentor this time.

Lerato's mind went blank for a moment as the gun pointed down at Refentše's skull . . .

The gunman moved backwards until he reached the window. He lifted up the corner of the curtain ever so slightly. He then moved closer again, towards Jack this time.

'Take off that shit over there!' – pointing with the gun at the telephone booth that was in the bar.

With one mighty attempt Jack pulled the handset off violently, so that he held it and its cord in his hand while the empty booth remained there by itself.

Lerato coughed again. Another suppressed cough. She waited for the gunshot. But just as worrying for her was the thought that something was sure to be done to her before the gunshot . . .

Their tormentor went back to the window and repeated his exercise of looking out. Whatever was happening outside did not progress at a speedy pace. The man came back to them again. He opened a can of the beer that Refentše had just bought.

The door opened slightly, and something was thrown into the bar. The man picked it up.

'You remain as you are until I come back. Which could be any time! Any silly movements from anyone and you'll serve as the example to the rest that I'm not here to play.'

He went out, and just as soon came back in . . . before Lerato could manage to whisper to Refentše to take the orders as they came, if only for her sake.

The man seemed to be satisfied with their behaviour.

'Good students!' he observed. 'Don't worry. As long as there are no monkey tricks, you will remain safe. All we came here for is the university car. Just be good students. Do not die for things that don't belong to you. We only came for the car that belongs to whites. Or is there any white student here?' he asked rhetorically.

His 'Don't worry . . . ' made Lerato the more uneasy. Her male companions might be spared being shot dead, she thought. But the man's words echoed the words that had announced the beginning of her friend's real ordeal. She saw her friend's story happening in this university residence, which she had always thought to be entirely safe. Or, at least, much safer than the streets of her township, Alexandra. Now it was clear to her that fleshy guns could be brandished anywhere.

Lerato could not swallow past the huge lump that stuck in her throat, making breathing almost impossible. The gunshot that presently exploded somewhere off the university premises made her eyes squeeze shut in anticipation. The gunman went out, repeating his order that they were to remain as they were and his threat that whoever disobeyed would serve as an example to the rest.

Lerato still had difficulty breathing even when, a long while after the gunman's departure, another student opened the unlocked door to the bar, and was surprised – and somewhat amused – to find them celebrating Amabokoboko's victory in their singular fashion, lying face down on the floor.

Refentše's Ordeal

Refentše wanted to laugh. That was before he realised that he was in grave danger. There was something rather strange about three men in balaclavas, pointing guns at him. He had never thought that his existence could threaten anyone.

It was on the day the South African team won the Rugby World Cup. Refentše and his friends watched the match on TV that afternoon, at a friend's flat in Hillbrow. None of them was a great fan of rugby. It was just that there was something thrilling, even if only temporarily, about identifying with Amabokoboko, as the South African rugby team, the Springboks, was sometimes fondly called. This was a team that, more than any other, was associated in their minds with the apartheid era. Now, with the government's rhetoric of a 'rainbow nation', Amabokoboko was supposedly one of the most important symbols of reconciliation and goodwill, and Rolihlahla Mandela could be seen in an Amabokoboko jersey when they played for the country. Refentše and his friends were now drunk, having bought loads of dumpies so that they would not have to go out while the game was still on.

After the match, they decided that they would join the noisy crowds in the streets of Hillbrow. While there, they decided that it would be even better to go to Johannesburg College of Education, where many rugby supporters, real as well as feigned, had been watching the match on big screens.

It was while on their way to the College that Refentše separated from his friends. He intended to buy meat. He invited the friends to join him for the usual supper of maize meal, meat and sauce – and, naturally, more drinks – when they were tired of the noise at the College. On arriving at his university residence at Parktown Village, only five minutes walk from the College, he prepared the meal that he had promised. While the maize meal was cooking on the stove, he dashed out to the Village bar to stock up with beer.

That was where the whole problem began.

It was not very bright in the bar. The main lights were switched off and the only lighting issued forth from the TV screen. There were only three other customers in the bar. Lerato and two fellow students whom Refentše did not know well sat close to the TV set. Jack stood behind the counter, from where he was selling the beer and watching TV as well. They were arguing about who the player of the day was in the rugby match.

Refentše greeted them, and after exchanging a few pleasantries with Lerato, he approached Jack.

'Two cases of cans, please,' he said. Jack asked what the occasion was.

'We have won, brother! That's it! Those New Zealanders thought that they owned this game of rugby. We have won!'

Jack smiled as he served Refentše. He could read from Refentše's tone that the match was not the most important occasion for drinking, if it could be called an occasion at all. Or maybe it was not that he could read what Refentše said, but rather that he knew he would have come to buy large quantities of beer, regardless. Some people said that the main reason Refentše did not have a girlfriend at the university, unusual for a man of his age, was that books and beer came first in the depths of his heart. Women, it was said, perhaps only came second. Or did not count at all. Some said that was why he had no love relationship with Lerato, despite the fact that, so the word went, she was clearly in love with him. Jack could not say for sure that Refentše's life could be explained so simply. But he could certainly testify to the number of times Refentše visited the bar. And to the large quantities Refentše usually bought there, even when, as was usually the case, there was no event to justify such spending.

As Refentše turned around to leave, he found himself facing the mouth of a gun, behind which was a balaclava, so that he could not see the face.

'Face down!'

Jack, Lerato and the other two students threw themselves down immediately. Refentše remained standing, wondering at it all. It had never occurred to him that one fateful day he might find himself held at gunpoint. It was like a movie without the big screen. Or even a small one, since these things are shown on TV so often these days.

'Come out from behind the counter!' Instructions hissed from the balaclava.

And to Refentše: 'Face down!'

The balaclava was slowly approaching him. As this second order hissed out from between the lips of the balaclava, another balaclava appeared at the slightly open door. It shifted over somewhat to allow a third one to appear, also pointing a gun at whoever might be in the bar. This third invader retreated as soon as he had appeared, and gently closed the door behind him.

The first invader was still approaching slowly, as if tiptoeing – maybe he was, Refentše was not quite sure – towards Refentše. He came very close. He patted Refentše on the shoulder.

'Don't try my patience . . . I said, "Face down!"'

It was the combination of the cold feel of the hand on his shoulder, the brutality of the voice hissing from the lips behind the balaclava, and the sharpened vision of the reality of the gun that spurred Refentše's brain to begin to do its work. Even then, it was not as quick as those who loved him could have wished. For, in the face of the odd prospect of his own impending death, Refentše found himself asking himself, with a sense of disbelief, whether all the wrongs that he had committed in his life justified this moment.

Unlike Jack, he did not hurl himself onto the cold tiles immediately. He walked, as if in an uneasy dream, towards the carpeted area, where Lerato and the others were lying. He made himself comfortable there. At least, as comfortable as one could be when death was looking one in the eyes, and you did not quite know how you had earned the impending death.

'Where is Jack?'

'Here.' Jack's voice was faint.

Refentše's thoughts shifted to concentrate on Jack. He wondered what personal grudges Jack, who was the most unrowdy person known to him in the whole Village, could have incurred with these gun-toting fellows.

'Where are the car keys?'

'Here.' Again, faintly.

'Throw them in front of you!'

Refentše looked at Jack as he stood up on his knees, feeling in his pocket for the keys. He was relieved for Jack's sake, although not without the disturbing misgiving that that was not all the gunmen wanted.

These, Refentše thought, were no ordinary robbers. How did they know that Jack had the university car keys? Had they organised with someone from within – a fellow student maybe, or, better still, a more knowledgeable university staff member? Perhaps they even knew exactly who Jack was, and were merely asking their questions for fun?

Jack used the car occasionally, on weekends, to carry beer from the brewery to the Village bar. On these occasions, he would also take advantage of his use of the car to visit his girlfriend and, often, bring her along to the Village. She was fortunately not with him this time, however.

Jack threw the keys down in front of him, towards the invader. The second invader picked them up. Apparently having decided that the students were harmless, the second invader said to his companion, 'Keep order!' and went out.

The first invader stayed behind.

Jack moved slightly, in order to make himself more comfortable. The gun pointed in his direction instantly.

Refentše's stomach tightened . . .

Lerato coughed. A stifled kind of cough that brought no soothing thoughts to Refentše's already sweating brain. It would be her turn now, he thought. He found himself reviewing his life quite quickly. It just flashed whole, with the speed of lightning, before him. Even in that brief moment of review, he found the chance to regret that Lerato was going to die, and he would follow suit, before he could tell her how much he loved her. His suddenly sober state – it was as if he had not drunk a thing not so long ago – did not make his fears and regrets more endurable.

He listened with dismay to the jubilant voices in the street, as people sang 'Amabokoboko aya phumelela . . . '

Presently the gun pointed at him again.

'Switch that shit off!' The gun pointed to the TV set this time.

Refentše stood up, gradually. He had already given himself and his companions up for dead. He walked slowly, hoping that the slowness of his movements would speed up the visitation of the first bullet into his skull.

He switched the shit off. Guided in the dimness by the lights outside the bar, he went back to his former place.

'Not there, cheeky bastard! Come over here.'

He stood up again. As he approached his tormentor, a thought flashed swiftly across his mind. What if he kicked hard at his tormentor's stomach? With his boots on, the result could be impressive.

But then he thought of the other two men. It was disturbing that he did not know exactly where they were. For the university car had not moved off yet; at least, there had not been any sound to suggest that it had. The men must still be on the premises. Refentše went down again, right at the feet of his tormentor this time.

The gunman moved backwards until he reached the window. He lifted up the corner of the curtain ever so slightly. He then moved closer again, towards Jack this time.

'Take off that shit over there!' – pointing with the gun at the telephone booth that was in the bar.

Refentše was later to admire the ingenuity of Jack's mind, as well as the strength of his muscles. With one attempt he had successfully pulled off the handset so violently that he held it and its severed cord in his hand, while the empty booth remained there by itself.

Lerato coughed again. A suppressed cough. Once more, Refentše's stomach tightened. He was afraid that Lerato's inconvenient cough was more than a robber would bear with. His review of his life resumed, at a quicker pace than before. He regretted that Lerato's cold was not being merciful to her. Even in such hard circumstances.

Their tormentor, however, said nothing. He did not even point his gun at Lerato. Instead, he went back to the window and repeated his exercise of looking out. Refentše was glad. It would have been doubly painful for him to be tormented himself, and to have to witness his sweetheart-to-be enduring the same torment.

What was going on in Lerato's heart and mind during these trying moments was unknown to Refentše. What he did know was that he had not yet told her that he loved her. He had always intended to tell her – each day he promised himself to do it before the sunset of the following day. But every day brought with it an increased dread of rejection. And, therefore, his haunted silence remained.

Whatever was happening outside did not progress at a speedy pace. The gunman came back to their side of the room again. He opened a can of the beer that Refentše had just bought. Refentše would gladly have offered the whole lot if he could only be persuaded that after his gesture of generosity the man would leave them in peace. As it was, however, he hated the man for opening this one can. The man drank it down quite quickly. One, two gulps and it was gone. He opened another one . . . The certainty of death did not stop Refentše's bitterness from mounting.

The door opened slightly. Something was thrown into the bar. The man picked it up.

'You remain as you are until I come back. Which could be any time! Any silly movements from anyone and you'll serve as an example to the rest that I'm not here to play.'

He went out, and almost immediately came back, before Refentše could reach any conclusion as to the man's voice and accent, which did not sound too unfamiliar. His thoughts fell into disarray at the man's re-entrance. Just as well that he had not stayed away long, Refentše thought to himself. For he had been about to stand up and leave.

Earlier, as Refentše had stood up to switch off the TV set, he had heard his friends' voices outside, singing 'Amabokoboko aya phumelela . . . '

They were chanting their way to his room, only to discover that he was not there. He remembered the food he had left cooking on the stove. The thought that someone might detect the smell as his food started to burn, and go to check in the communal kitchen, offered no consolation whatever. His friends, on finding him not there, would have most likely used the other exit point on leaving. He thought he could still hear their voices, only much more distantly now.

The gunman seemed to be satisfied with the behaviour of his victims.

'Good students!' he observed when he came back in.

Again Refentše started to wonder about the voice. The accent sounded rather forced to him. He was almost positive that he was familiar with the speech patterns of this person, despite the forced accent.

'Don't worry. As long as there are no monkey tricks, you will remain safe. All we came here for is the university car. Just be good students. Do not die for things that don't belong to you. We only came for the car that belongs to whites. Or is there any white student here?' the man asked rhetorically.

Refentše thought about the exorbitant fees that he and all the other students were paying. His thoughts moved on to contemplate the uncertainty of their redemption. He visualised, in his mind's eye, the agonised face of his mother on receiving the news of his death; the faces of his two cousins, the police officer who had accommodated and provided him with food in his Hillbrow flat, before he was able to secure his university bedsitting room, and Konketšo, the loving cousin who provided some back-up to her policeman brother. The thoughts came in the form of quick, sharp mind pictures that belittled the efforts of the most advanced of cameras. Then, as if to underscore his visions, a gunshot exploded from the outside. 'Amabokoboko aya phumelela . . . ' stopped abruptly. The silence that followed was a long one. When Refentše's mind quit its blankness and returned to the bar, the silence was still there, in all its impenetrability, as was the thick presence of the man in the balaclava.

And 'Don't worry . . . ' rattled in Refentše's skull as if the gun had exploded on the Village premises . . .

My Pa Se Kind[1]

It's you
my pa se kind
i have been wondering
& wandering
knowing full well
the pain
of lost love
but now you're found
my ma se kind[2]
you're found . . .
you're . . .
you're found romancing the towers
of hillbrow

1. My father's child.
2. My mother's child.

Occasion For Brooding

He has already swallowed a few dumpies, as he often does on Fridays. And on other days. His memory of Tshepo competes for his attention with thoughts of what he could say to his mother, now. And to his friends? Everyone was now surely in a position to say to him:

'There is a Jo'burg woman for you!'

Throughout the day, at the university, he has suffered visions of sharp gazes focused on him, and of voices reminding him of what his people had always known would be the inevitable outcome of his stubbornness. The gazes and voices had multiplied in his imagination, becoming sharper and louder by the second. There were moments when he would shrug with fright as he fixed faces, familiar village faces, to the gazes and voices.

His main wish was to retreat, to withdraw from the pandemonium. The worst torment was the keen knowledge that what he conjured was what he would see and hear in reality, sooner or later. Every moment that elapsed was another mighty step towards the ushering in of this dreaded moment. Not having chosen to be born, he feels it is regrettable that he would not now be left alone to choose how to live.

Entangled in this maze of brooding, he forgets that he himself had once done something similar to Sammy. That was about a year back. The secret had been well sheltered.

For now, Refentše is simply overwhelmed by the painful freshness of his morning findings. He wonders if Tshepo was not truly lucky to have passed away before he got too disappointed with life.

He lifts the dumpy up to his mouth again. The beer is bereft of its usual refreshing taste. He looks at the setting sun. No warmth there, either. Just the orange at the edge of the clouds that hide it somewhat. Everything is too quiet for his liking.

He walks slowly into the flat. The music is still playing softly. *See the world through the eyes of a child . . .* His favourite piece. By Stimela.

He presses the volume button. Again. And again . . . until the volume is at full blast.

He unlocks the door that leads out of the flat into the corridor. *See the world through the eyes of a child . . .*

He goes back to the balcony. Sits on the balcony wall. Takes another sip of the beer, wondering why it tastes so strange today. Looking into the street, twenty levels down from where he is sitting, he sees a woman taking a dog for a walk. The sight reminds him of a story Sammy had once told him during one of their drinking sessions. It was about their friend's dog, Danger.

One day, the story goes, Danger was chasing a mouse. The mouse beat Danger to its hole. While in the hole, it saw Danger blocking the opening with his snout, sniffing angrily as if to follow. Overcome with fright and frustration, the mouse ran out of the hole, straight into Danger's mouth.

There had been nothing to suggest that the coming funeral would become one of the most talked about events, not only in Tiragalong and its neighbourhood, but also in such distant places as Nobody and Boyne. Nothing, that is, except that the gruesome death of such a successful youth was enough in itself to make it the talk of the village. Because no one knew the exact cause of the death, creative minds found no difficulty in divining it. Refentše's friend Sammy was known to be one of the very few villagers who took a sympathetic view of the calamity.

'For a person of Refentše's calibre,' Sammy said, 'whose outlook on life was always positive, the cause must have been very deep indeed.'

Refentše's mother could only brood over her son's death. It never occurred to her that she had killed her own son. She only meant to show him the light. The son was in search of the light, too. He found his own light in the end. This, the mother could not comprehend.

'Some things are just too baffling,' she said with much sadness.

For those with imagination and wagging tongues the issue was simple. Here was an educated youth who could not think beyond himself, beer and Jo'burg women. As was well known in the village, Jo'burg women could frustrate a man. Refentše had often been advised to keep away from them. The words went into his head through one ear and, just as quickly, went out the other. As always happens to those who mistake a lion's mouth for a playing field, he got chewed by the lion.

But his mother's strange behaviour forced even Refentše's detractors to change their minds about where the blame lay.

'Surely Refentše was bewitched by his own mother?' the villagers said.

It was not that the mother had ever been thought of as a witch. But the kind of conduct that she was now displaying was associated with witchcraft.

The oldest villagers used to tell stories of witches who fell into the graves of the people they had killed. Only two instances of such bizarre acts were known, both of which had happened in the distant past. Neither of them had happened in Tiragalong.

One took place at Nobody, and the other at neighbouring Nnoko, which shares boundaries with Tiragalong. The two witches, it was said, were newcomers to the art. So their medicines overcame them with their strength and turned against them. Or, it was said, the deceaseds' Ancestors were very angry and vented their rage on the witches. Nobody knew what the real truth was. But all knew that it was unheard of to fall into a dead person's grave. Doctors were consulted in the villages concerned and the two witches were confirmed as such. They were later thrown out of their respective villages.

So when Refentše's mother fell into her son's grave on that hot Saturday morning – as she was throwing into it a handful of soil to bid him goodbye – the village was reminded of the two stories.

What frustrated the village was the knowledge that she had clearly killed her own son, using medicines. It was difficult to know what to do with her. In ordinary circumstances she would have trodden the same path as that travelled by Tshepo's murderess.

But on this occasion the Comrades were not in agreement. Half of them said that, in killing her own son, she had done harm to no one but herself. Killing her own son, who was going to assist her in life, was like committing suicide. It was not something that society should spend sleepless nights over. Every villager knew that the cry of a person who commits suicide is a drum; when it plays, people dance.

The other half said that Refentše was going to bring advancement to the whole village. His death was in many ways the death of this advancement. The village thus had every responsibility to protect itself from the ill will of such night prowlers as his mother.

In the end agreement could not be reached. Because the village was going to have to explain its decision to the cruel Mankweng police, it was decided that such accounting would be jeopardised by the split.

Refentše is alone on the balcony of his flat in Hillbrow. Or perhaps he is not alone. Besides beer, Refentše's other companion is the fond memory of Tshepo, and his thoughts of the pain families have to continue to endure because of the sudden deaths of those who should be in a position to relieve them of their poverty.

Refentše and Tshepo attended the same high school. He was in his first year there when Tshepo read for his matric. Tshepo was the first pupil from the school, the only high school in Tiragalong, to go and study at a university in the South. On receiving his results he was struck by fatal lightning. Grief sent his mother to join him in the world of the Ancestors.

What pained Refentše very much was that Tshepo's death meant the loss of a role model. Tshepo was not only the first in the village to go to the university in the South. He was about to become the only teacher, except for the principal, who had a degree. All the other teachers had teachers' diplomas from the colleges in the homeland of Lebowa. It was going to be a real change having a teacher whose education transcended Verwoerdian food for thought.

To some of his former teachers, this was not altogether good news. For they knew that their teaching experience was not necessarily going to secure them a higher status than him in the future.

But with Refentše the case was different. He had nothing to lose from Tshepo's success, after all.

Refentše was just about to enrol for his first year at the same university when Tshepo died. Tshepo had told him about the advantages of going to study there.

'If you work hard enough,' he would encourage his younger companion, 'you could pass with flying colours. And get a scholarship! Some of the lecturers are also very supportive. One of them helped me to get my essay published.'

Tshepo had something to show for his work. An essay published while he was still in his second year! In his final year he published a short story. He always told Refentše that he was heading for bigger things. Surely Refentše should be equally ambitious!

That was how Refentše came to apply for admission at the institution of higher alienation, as he subsequently came to call it. Tshepo had not romanticised the nature of the institution in any way. But until his own experiences there, Refentše had not quite believed that Tshepo and the other students from impoverished educational backgrounds could suffer so much at the university. As they say in Tiragalong, to be told is to be deprived; whereas seeing for oneself is like eating. So it was with Refentše.

Refentše first came to Johannesburg in January 1991. He was an optimistic youth, who had passed his matric subjects well. Not quite with distinction, but well enough to be admitted unconditionally to enrol for his degree of Bachelor of Arts. Initially, he wanted to study Commerce. But his Mathematics question paper was a bit uncooperative, as his final results showed. Not knowing what else to do, he enrolled for the Arts degree. He had vaguely thought of becoming a journalist, or an editor – although he had no idea what editors did. Since he could not study his first choice, Commerce, he thought he could pursue the dreams of his childhood. For he was in lower primary school when he first encountered the word 'editor'.

After seeking advice – he was always told by his loving mother how important it is for people not to pretend to know – he resolved to study literature. With literature courses and a course or two in the Social

Sciences, he was told, he should be in a position to become an editor or journalist. Or even both!

So he looked attentively at the year's timetable to check that his subjects did not clash.

English Studies . . . He hoped that Enid Blyton would be on the reading list. He had literally grown up on Enid Blyton. Second choice . . . ; it clashed with English Studies. Then . . . He saw something called African Studies on the timetable. He loved Kgadime Matsepe with every drop of passion in his heart. He was the finest Sepedi novelist Refentše had ever read. Not that he had read much Sepedi literature. African literature written in Sepedi was not readily available in their tiny school library. And, with the raving poverty at home, owning a book was, for him, quite a luxury. Anyway, because of too little information on what students did in their African Studies classes, and telling himself that for the first time he would be able to study Sepedi literature without the inhibitions of the secondary school syllabus, he enrolled.

As for the other subjects, he had a terribly limited interest in them. They simply completed the empty blocks on his forms.

He passed his first year unconvincingly. By the second year he had picked up a bit. He eventually qualified for a postgraduate degree, after making his brain sweat a lot. For not only was he struggling to bridge the gap between his secondary education and university learning, but there were many other problems. Some of his lecturers were the embodiment of rudeness. Dr Lewi was one such lecturer. Three moments stand out in his memory of Lewi.

One day in his first year, his university friend – or, rather, fellow sufferer – failed his assignment. Lewi had a way with words. He wrote his comments on the poor soul's assignment: 'You have to earn marks. You do not just find them lying in a tray!'

Dr Lewi could not be bothered to find out where the students' problems lay. He was not bothered that many of them were the product of the poor educational system known as 'Bantu Education'. His view was that only those who were up to the toughness of university learning should be admitted. Even if this meant the near exclusion of all black students. His belief was firm, as any number of his past students could testify.

There was a second occasion, when Lewi had charged another classmate with looking at him with 'eyes of ignorance'. This particular classmate was a frail personality. She had cried silently while a few male students enjoyed the joke. On that day, Refentše had been the only other black student in the discussion group. He'd sympathised with Lerato a lot. More so as he feared that he was likely to be the next victim of Dr Lewi's linguistic skills. But that had not happened . . . then. He had to wait two more months before his turn came.

Refentše received a letter from Lewi, who was also the course supervisor. It said that he had not attended the required minimum of discussion groups. He would therefore not be allowed to sit the June examinations.

Refentše knew it wasn't true. It could not be! He was certain he had attended far more tutorials than the stipulated minimum. Fortunately the letter also indicated that it was open to correction.

Appreciating the fairness of the last point, he visited the supervisor. As Lewi's office door was always shut and his hearing was not good, Refentše had to knock hard. Lewi shouted an irritable 'Come in!'

Refentše opened the door. He greeted timidly. The office looked impressive, even when viewed through Refentše's apprehensive eyes. Shelves and shelves that almost touched the roof were packed with big books, old and new, in all shapes and sizes. Refentše could not help feeling that Lewi must be a very strong man indeed to have read all those books and still remain sane enough to be able to teach.

'How can I help you, young man?' came the rather hoarse voice of Lewi.

Refentše, not having a sufficient supply of confidence in his English skills, simply fumbled in his pocket. He produced the condemning document, and handed it to his lecturer. Lewi gave it a quick glance. He consulted his file briefly. A sneer grew on his face.

'Young man!' Lewi's voice barked, as he banged on the table. It was so unexpected that Refentše started. 'Young man, according to our records, your attendance at the discussion groups has been less than sparkling! Can you tell us why that is so?'

That is not so! stuck in Refentše's throat.

'But . . . ' he stammered instead. Before he could find the right words, Lewi intimated that he was not going to argue with first years.

In that moment of frustration Refentše stood up. He feared for his life on remembering, when he was already two offices away, that he had not shut Lewi's office door behind him.

The alienation caused to first years by the likes of Lewi was difficult to overcome, even with the support of fellow students and a few more humane lecturers, who did not believe that their jobs at the university were simply limited to research.

It was worse for those like Refentše. Every time he was treated badly in that way, he would remember his mother . . . the poverty . . . the two huts in the homestead which were threatening to collapse at any time. The possibility that he might not be able to return to the university due to financial difficulties haunted him constantly. No, it was not easy at all!

The following year he had to apply for a study loan. The same thing happened in his third and fourth years of study. He only received his scholarship when reading for his Master's degree the year after. That was an acknowledgement, finally, of his ability.

He thought now of the late Tshepo, of how his death had deprived Refentše of the chance to celebrate with his homeboy. For, like Tshepo, Refentše was busy making a name for himself, and for Tiragalong.

On seeing his amazing progress, Refentše's lecturers constantly told him, in his third year of study, that he would make a brilliant academic. When he was reading for his Honours, one lecturer even allowed him to take a tutorial, once. The experience was so exciting that in that moment, Refentše witnessed his lecturers' prophetic words become hard fact. All thoughts of journalism or editing as a career evaporated through his skull into the open air.

At the time he began to lecture, he could not cope financially. About a quarter of his salary went into repaying his student loans. He realised that he had agreed to contracts that demanded that he now pay more than he could afford. The contracts were not explained to him the way that he now knew they should have been. His limited English vocabulary and innocence as to how contracts worked did not stand him in good stead. It was an unsettling discovery that he had, in fact, authorised his own suffering. Another quarter of his salary was devoured by the taxperson. Yet another quarter disappeared in the form of monthly rentals. After paying his furniture instalments, he was left with too little for subsistence. Too little even for himself, that is. He had to live on lice, as they say in Tiragalong. And what with family obligations and other forms of pressure, he could think of no way out.

What really depressed him was that his mother failed to understand his problems. And why should she? Had she not spent every cent she could lay her hands on on her beloved son? The exorbitant tuition fees. The unfriendly transport fares. The new clothes. The everything.

'Refentše is too inconsiderate,' she said. 'And too extravagant.'

His trusted cousin, Konketšo had told her that Refentše lived for beer. And for Jo'burg girls.

In imparting this piece of wisdom to her aunt, the cousin was motivated by both her fear for Refentše's safety with these Jo'burg girls, and concern for her aunt's peace of mind, which could only be achieved through a severing of Refentše's love relationship.

As if the two reasons were insufficient, she also had to satisfy her passion for personal revenge. Since Refentše had invited the bone of his heart to stay with him in his flat, Konketšo had increasingly felt her own influence over Refentše wane. In the good old times, she had been able to simply walk into the flat and serve herself whatever she liked from the refrigerator, which was often nearly empty, without having to ask for permission. Now, Refentše suggested to her that such behaviour undermined the status of the new woman of the house.

Konketšo could not allow herself to be trampled down by this newcomer in Refentše's life. That she was a newcomer was in itself bad enough. That she was also a Johannesburger could only smear her already ugly image with grimy mud in the eyes of Konketšo. She wondered how her beloved cousin could allow himself to be controlled by a girl. She put her wonderment into strong words that indicated to Refentše that his mother would undoubtedly know of this love relationship at the earliest possible time. These strong words expressed Konketšo's new-found doubt at Refentše's integrity, while simultaneously spiting the newcomer.

Konketšo said loudly that her aunt had merely accompanied other women to the clinic; while they returned with babies wrapped with warmth in their tender arms, she had returned empty-handed. Now, in her old age, she would have no son to take good care of her. So it was that she resolved and threatened to alert her aunt to the impending fate that awaited her, when she went home the following weekend.

Refentše knew his cousin well enough to know that there would be difficult times ahead, beginning from the very moment his and his mother's eyes met on the occasion of their next meeting.

The danger that Konketšo envisaged found concrete expression in the fact that Refentše was penniless when he went home, only two weeks after payday. He admitted that he had a lover from the townships of the city – but not from Hillbrow, whose reputation for prostitution and crime kept on ascending to the clear skies of Tiragalong, as migrants brought into the village new wild stories every time they returned home. Refentše made his admission plainly. That, really, was what dealt him the blow.

Yet, he could not see how he, who loved his mother dearly, could bring himself to lie to her. The truth had to come out. The choice imposed on him by the truth was exacting.

There was a general belief in the village of Tiragalong that Jo'burg women were nothing but parasites. The basis of this popular opinion was not quite clear to Refentše, if it was to anyone else. Perhaps it was because a number of men who went to work in the South often fell in love with women there, and subsequently sent too little back to their families in the rural site. Perhaps the few who actually married the Johannesburgers were left destitute, without possessions. Refentše knew of one such case in the village. The man lost his property in a divorce case. Whatever the true roots of the belief, Refentše's mother shared wholeheartedly in it.

When Refentše suggested to his mother that rural women were, in fact, no better than the Jo'burg women, all she said was: 'You break with her, or you are no longer my son!'

Refentše was startled. For the first time in the twenty-four years of his life, he learnt that his mother could shut her ears to his words. Not only that. She could also shut the doors of her brain to reason, even in the face of hard fact. After all, his mother knew well that her son had failed in relationships with the young women of Tiragalong.

On the first occasion, the would-be lover told Refentše that he was quite a loveable chap. But she let honesty take the prize: 'You do not own a car!' she said to him.

Refentše had been left to reflect painfully on the amount of time he had spent trying to bring her to the point where she could openly express the contents of her heart. He had interpreted her silence all along, her apparent unwillingness to tell him once and for all what the state of her heart was, as one of those weaknesses he should expect from women. He derived no comfort from learning that, in the long run, silence can be simply a way of avoiding stabbing at the hearts of those you care about.

Armed with this fresh piece of wisdom, Refentše was from that day onwards extremely sensitive to the fact of his family's poverty.

Confronted with the vision of his powerlessness and worthlessness, he had even considered suicide. When he told Sammy about his disappointment, though deliberately omitting to mention his gloomy intentions, Sammy had merely laughed away this woman's honesty as a sign that she did not really love him. He reminded Refentše that his education was sure to lift him out of poverty soon. There were a number of examples in the neighbouring villages of people who rose from the dust of their parents' huts to live in big houses and drive good cars. Sammy, with his patience, dived into the list of these villagers. After which he reminded Refentše once more that love and a car did not really make an ideal couple for any villager of worth. They were fine if they came your way. But you did not make yourself miserable because they did not.

The way Sammy had laughed away the thought that love and a car could go together forced Refentše to reflect that Tiragalong would have a poor opinion of him if it were to discover why he decided to commit suicide. He was not one of those people who simply said that death was death and ended there. Refentše's sense of dignity required that people should also speak well of him while he rested in the grave. These thoughts put him under pressure not to talk about his contemplated suicide to anyone.

Even with the new pressures infused into his life, Sammy's optimism about the future gave Refentše a reason for holding onto life for as long as he could. And in that way, saved his dignity from sinking into the muddy pool of suicide. Refentše's new task, since then, had been to uproot the poverty at home as soon as he could. It was with this ambition constantly flooding his mind that he worked hard and with perseverance in the subsequent years of his student life. And it was this renewed hope in life that led him to another lover.

The second lover, he discovered two months into the relationship, had at least four other lovers. Or, rather, sexual partners. He learnt this from the New Release, as such partners are sometimes known.

He met the Latest Release by chance when on his way back from the university one day. It was during university holidays and he had gone in to complete his research essay. On his return the following day, the minibus taxi had problems. Their journey was delayed by no less than three hours. On arriving in Pietersburg, he found that there were no taxis at that time to Tiragalong or its neighbourhood.

Since the village was about forty-five kilometres from the town, he decided to hitch his way home. Walking would have been too much of a bother. Besides, it was late. Everyone knew that Nobody, through which he would have to pass, was full of tsotsis. Who wanted to die just when he was about to complete all the requirements for his BA Honours degree, especially after the years of terrible alienation and hard work? If there were any such people, Refentše was decidedly not one of them.

He waited on the boundary of the town, on the road to Mankweng. For about an hour he had leant against the signpost that read 'Lebowa Boundary' on the side facing the town, and 'Pietersburg Grens' on the other side. A car came to a halt.

'Want a lift? To . . . ?'

'Tiragalong.'

'Throw yourself in, brother.'

He lost no time at all. The driver was friendly and talkative. He told Refentše of his sexual exploits. And other trivialities.

'Yes, I know your village quite well. I used to be famous with the girls there. Not that I am no longer famous. You know Refilwe?'

Refentše nodded.

'She is my cherry. I only won her last week. It is nothing to boast about, really. Everyone knows she is fairly open-thighed. Want a beer?'

Refentše shook his head.

'Just to give you an idea of what I mean, she has got three other boyfriends . . . '

Refentše tried to suppress his emotions. He was usually calm and gentle. And generous of spirit. But this frightening piece of news was more than he could cope with. The driver kept his eyes glued to the rough, stony road while the story continued to flow from his eager tongue with unfailing consistency. The dimness of the light in the car reassured Refentše somewhat that the driver, if he chanced to glance at him, would not see much of his facial expression. It was a small consolation that helped to make him manage his anger for the duration of the journey.

He paid a reasonable fare for his ride. The news was, of course, for free.

When he met his lover the following day, Refentše passed on greetings from the Latest Release, who had not really appointed him as messenger. For Refentše's benefit, the lover wondered aloud who this person could be. Refentše did not claim to know him. He only hinted that he knew a lot more than she might guess. He told her, for example, about her partner at Nnoko.

Fearing that Refentše might grow irritated by her pretences, she decided to reveal everything about her relationships. She hoped that he would forgive her. Which he did. And, on that note, he left her to herself and the care of the other partners.

His mother knew all this. She might not have known about the once-contemplated suicide. Maybe she did not need to know about it, he thought. Maybe parents did not have to know such things before they could listen to their children with two open ears. The thought mingled with a persistent question: What was so special about rural women that supposedly made them better lovers than those in Johannesburg? After all, he wondered, when people talked about Johannesburgers, were they not, in fact, simply referring to people from the rural areas, who were, like himself, in search of greener pastures? And when men were generous enough to give their all to their extramarital partners, was that not what the provisions of greener pastures were partly about?

'You leave this woman, or you are no longer my son . . . ' His mother's voice, engraved in his mind, disturbed the already confused flow of his thoughts, only to leave him with an even more intense form of brooding.

Things really came to a head when Refentše became the talk of the village. He learnt from Sammy, who had gone home one weekend, of all the bad things being said about him. How he did not love his mother. How his mother was suffering as if her son were not a lecturer. And many other such things.

Refentše was thoroughly humiliated when he went home the next time. A number of young women, including those whose morals were poor by village standards, gave him a piece of their minds. Even the honest woman, his first lover, whom Refentše had never really stopped loving, talked spiritedly about a 'country bumpkin' who mistook himself for a city 'wisey'.

When he once more failed to secure an open ear from his mother on that occasion, Refentše resolved not to return home again.

But there were people from Tiragalong, working in Johannesburg, who were prepared to come and pester him at his flat. Not only were they prepared – they actually did it! Even his friends, with the exception of Sammy, who knew his problems, said Refentše was wrong not to support his poor mother. He could not go about discussing his domestic affairs with everyone. Their criticism was largely ill-informed. He understood, and did not hold it against them.

In the end, he found things out for himself. Nothing was blown into his ears by any too-loud-mouthed winds.

He had forgotten one of his important documents behind at the flat. After the first two lectures of the day he went back home to fetch the document, for he could not do without it. Thinking that the bone of his heart might still be asleep, he did not knock. He simply unlocked the door and marched into the flat.

He found Lerato still in bed. With her eyes and legs open, and Sammy, moaning . . .

When I Am Awake

i read in the darkness
of my wandering gloom
initially
i thought we meant it
biting gently
at each other's necks
& saying
even the el nino
frustrating farmers
is a child to our towering love
no doubt
love we had in abundance
no doubt
bone of my heart
but like the limpopo
after torrents
of rain relieved
those brooding heavens
the love overflowed
the river vomited
its excesses
into the guts
of the deprived souls
pining for love
in quartz street
bone of my heart
you were not alone
in this expansive generosity
i too
dished out smiles

like the ember
does on autumn
mornings
rising with compassionate stare
from the eastern mountains
now
here i am
reading in the dark
with seamus deane
trying mightily
to read my reading
& my brooding mind
& turbulent passions
evading the gaze
of searching eyes
i'm reading in the dark
reading your absence
wondering what you're reading now
though knowing
you too
must be reading in the dark
wondering what we thought we were doing
dishing out love
as if it were
food

Fountains Of Brooding

A matchstick thrown into the hut from which the shrill screams of Refentše's mother can be heard falls onto a piece of cloth that is wet with petrol. Once more the Comrades of Tiragalong have taken off from their bodies the dress of cowardice, and are now displaying their bravery, solidarity and co-operation in solving the main problem of the village. Their cause has the support of Comrades from neighbouring villages – Nnoko, which shares the south-east boundary with Tiragalong; Magokobung to the east; Makgwareng to the north; as well as Phuti, which stretches from the north-west to the west of Tiragalong. Were the first village to the south not a bit too far, the Comrades there would probably also have come chanting freedom songs in corrupted isiZulu, to assist their fellow sufferers in Tiragalong. For witchcraft is quite a problem in this part of the planet. Especially in the tiniest of the villages, Tiragalong itself.

The problem caused by the incident at Refentše's graveside, which has led to much constipation in the minds of the Comrades, has finally been resolved. The split within the Comrade circles has been overcome by sharp intellects, and nearly all the young voices in Tiragalong are shouting in unison, as they did a few years ago when they necklaced the old woman to death for having sent lightning to strike Tshepo. Witchcraft shall be no more! Refentše's mother is now facing the music, as the somewhat educated youth put it.

Clouds of black smoke ascend the skies in great haste as the petrol catches the tiny flame from the matchstick. The clouds are much blacker than the brooding ones that brought the lightning that summoned Tshepo and, through grief, his mother, to the world of the Ancestors. They spread themselves to envelop the village with blackness. The green, lush grass, the big mealie plants in the fields, the beautiful greenness of the tree leaves, all the greenness in Tiragalong surrenders to the blackness of the smoke. It is as if the Gods have resolved, perhaps this once in a lifetime, to bring a miracle to the village and its neighbourhood in the form of black fog.

There is fog everywhere, spreading itself to embrace Nnoko, Magokobung, Makgwareng and Phuti, heading for where nobody knows, travelling much further than the fierce loudness of the Comrades' freedom songs could ever hope to reach.

Mahlodi, Refentše's mother, screams by herself from the heart of the raging flames because her companion, Phaswa, has died just before the burning could begin. When the Comrades went to summon him from his home he had shown signs of protest. In their impatience some of the Comrades had begun to stone him on the spot. By the time they reached Mahlodi's compound, his body was already giving signals of bidding the Comrades farewell. None of them noticed the signals. Or perhaps they did, but mostly had little interest in them. The sympathetic few were not able to display their compassion. A show of sympathy for night prowlers, especially in such trying times, was equivalent to whistling to death as it was absentmindedly passing you by.

In the end Phaswa departed, thus refraining from being turned into braaivleis while still alive. Mahlodi is once more deserted. She faces the music by herself. Gravesides! Dangerous places to be nearby on a hot Saturday morning.

It had begun as a rumour. Or maybe not quite rumour, for the gossips heard it from a reliable source. The source could not have been anyone but Refentše's youngest cousin, Leruo, who came to stay with Mahlodi soon after her son's suicide. The news, though so terribly unexpected, gave a powerful justification for the killing of Mahlodi.

Leruo was sitting in his hut, working on his composition. It was not the easiest thing to do. His ability lay more in figures than creative writing. Besides, the assignment itself was not the most exciting, given the topic: 'Our School . . . ' What could he do with such a topic, Leruo wondered? The school was small. It was poor, without impressive classrooms or a garden, and with teachers who were quite keen on using a stick on the pupils. They often quoted an English saying about the sparing of rods . . . or something similar. It would surely have been better if the school was Tiragalong High, and not Nnoko Secondary School, which the villagers seemed to have little interest in developing. For this reason, many parents in Nnoko sent their children to Tiragalong for their secondary education.

This line of positive thinking about Tiragalong High impressed itself strongly on Leruo's mind. But he could not think of Tiragalong High without remembering Refentše. Although still in Standard Six, Leruo understood enough of life to know that the way Refentše had died was unnatural. It was the kind of knowledge that was bound to distress him. Refentše was not just a cousin; he had also been a friend to Leruo.

There came a gentle knock on the door, which was met by an uninterested 'Come in' from Leruo. To his joy, in walked 'God's Blessing'. His friend, Thabo, had arrived much earlier than arranged.

'What are you doing working so late? You should be asleep by now!'

Leruo looked at Thabo. 'It's that fool Stick giving us homework on a Friday. As if we don't have better things to do. I want to get this done so that I have nothing to bother me for the rest of the weekend.'

Leruo scratched his head, and shook it slightly. With a hopeful smile he suggested: 'Maybe you can help?'

Thabo often had ideas. Also, he tended to be open-handed with them. So, together, the young pair worked through the assignment. It was about midnight when they completed it.

Thabo, whose parents were fairly rich and gave him pocket money, had brought with him the promised glue. Now was the moment to have a great time sniffing it. It must be good, for Leruo had heard Phaswa talk about it during the course of the afternoon. How he used to sniff it as a little boy. And how he would see things, of all sorts! What Leruo did not hear was that Phaswa was actually criticising the practice. Not that it would have made much difference to him, for what Leruo overheard was enough to tempt him anyway.

When he had told Thabo about Phaswa's stories, his friend also grew curious to taste what men had experienced in their younger days. He had offered to sacrifice his pocket money and use it to buy some glue. He and Leruo planned to meet in the course of the night, when Mahlodi was asleep.

Just before she went to bed, Mahlodi had gone into Leruo's hut to ask him something, and had been quite impressed to find the two boys doing homework on a Friday. Especially Friday evening, when less studious children were out playing in the streets in the bright moonlight. These two! Theirs was a rare kind of commitment, she repeated to herself numerous times.

Thabo woke up at about four in the morning. Looking out through the crack in the wall to check how dark it was, so that he could dash home before sunrise and ensure that his parents would not discover his absence, he saw Phaswa coming out of Mahlodi's hut. It seemed strange to him that old men should also sleep out. His father used to criticise such men for their boyish conduct. Thabo did not exclude the possibility that Phaswa could have fallen asleep while at his glue, as he and Leruo had just done. He was absorbed by this train of thought when Leruo moved slightly.

'No, Refentše!' came out of his mouth. His scream gave Thabo a fright. He shook Leruo violently and the latter woke up with a start. Leruo shook his head, rubbed his eyes, then unexpectedly gave another piercing scream and dashed for the door, which neither he nor Thabo had bothered to lock. He ran as if in fear for his life, all the while screaming: 'Leave me alone . . . leave me alone . . . !'

His hasty journey into the unknown was abruptly brought to an end by Phaswa, into whom he bumped in his flight.

Phaswa would have been worried that there was something seriously wrong with the boy had his nostrils not caught the telltale whiffs of glue that emanated from him as Leruo puffed and panted with fright, suspended in mid-air in Phaswa's huge, strong hands. He took the boy back to the hut.

Thabo was still there, baffled, but with sufficient presence of mind to snore noisily in the hope that Phaswa would not trouble him.

A day later, the Comrades met to take up again what they had previously failed to finish. When Mahlodi fell into Refentše's grave a short while before, the village accused her of being a witch. Because of similar incidents that had previously happened in other villages, they knew that such behaviour was associated with witchcraft. This time, there was no need to consult the doctors. It was now common knowledge that one could only fall into the deceased's grave if one had bewitched the deceased.

But the Comrades could not simply necklace Mahlodi to death as they wanted to, because of their fear of the Mankweng police. The real problem was that the Comrades were divided on whether to punish Mahlodi for practising the evil art. She had killed her own son and that was a family matter, said one section of the Comrades. While others said no, she had done Tiragalong a great disservice and deserved to be punished. Because of the split in ranks, they had decided to leave her alone. For it would have been impossible to justify the intimidation they would suffer at the hands of the police if they were not in agreement. As the elders say, lions that do not hunt together get outrun by a limping buffalo, and starve as a result.

Now the problem had been inadvertently resolved by Leruo.

'I understand your point well,' said Comrade Raditaba. 'But my point is not that we should punish her because she killed Refentše. That was her own son and we cannot involve ourselves in her family matters. What I am saying is that she clearly also killed Tshepo about five years ago. Surely we must bring an end to such behaviour? If we don't, then it will be our turn soon. Unless we all decide not to go off to learn in the South!'

'I support the Comrade over there. Remember, too, that we punished the wrong person for that first misdeed. Surely, if we can kill the innocent, then we have no reason not to kill the guilty?' It was Sammy who now spoke, Refentše's best friend.

As he said these words, his voice trembled with anger and his eyes were filled with tears. Even the most detached of the Comrades could not help being touched by his emotion. They were reminded of his obituary at Refentše's funeral.

As Refentše's friend he was allowed to talk at length about his friend's life. He emphasised the clear vision for the welfare of Tiragalong that Refentše had had. Equally, he emphasised how generous Refentše always was, so that his education was bound to benefit all in Tiragalong and the neighbourhood. He reminded them of the voluntary library work and teaching that Refentše had done for Tiragalong High since he commenced his studies at the university. What he said impressed strongly on all present that Refentše's suicide was, indeed, a loss for the village. He rounded off his speech with a suitable praise song for his friend's soul that was now resting in the world of the Ancestors.

What Sammy did not hint at in his speech was the possibility that Refentše might have committed suicide because Sammy himself and Refentše's lover, Lerato, despite the great love and respect they had for him, had nevertheless betrayed him. Refentše found them in his bedroom with their guilt still fresh on their hands on the morning of the fateful Friday when he had returned unexpectedly to his Hillbrow flat to pick up the document that he needed for a lecture he was about to give. The shock he received deprived him of words. He did not say anything to either of them, simply left for the campus to do his work. There, he was brought to the discovery that there were times when he was a useless teacher, given to dwelling more on thoughts about friendship and sex, than on books.

When he came back later that afternoon, the lover was not there. She feared that he might do something terrible to her. She used to remark to him that quiet people were dangerous, because you seldom knew what was on their minds. It was true that Refentše was the quiet type. But his mind was seldom eaten away by bitterness and ill will.

Sammy, also, did not come to have a drink with Refentše that Friday afternoon, as he usually did. He lacked the courage to apologise to his friend. He was not sure whether, even if he did decide to apologise, he would know exactly how to do it. Wrong words might lead him into a deep donga from which he would not necessarily be able to find his way out. He had risked Refentše's wrath. He had no desire to see it transformed into action.

So Refentše had his drink by himself that Friday afternoon. There was very little fun in it. It was at sunset when he finally found solace in jumping into the street from the balcony of his flat.

Sammy did not give so much as a hint of these events. As he sat down after his speech, voices shouted their support. Surely, the voices agreed, the Comrades could not allow that Tiragalong should lose people of substance just because of the madness of one old woman? In the end, the Comrades' wrath overcame their fear of the police. Creativity took its toll, as isiZulu once again got corrupted in the service of freedom.

It was a fulfilling day for Raditaba.

Raditaba and Phaswa were not friends. This was not just because Phaswa was old and Raditaba was a boy to him. Those who know these things say that Raditaba's father would have married Mahlodi, were it not for Phaswa. The two were lovers when Phaswa arrived as a migrant from the South, flashing money in Mahlodi's face as if it were mere sheets of paper. Raditaba's father was poor. As poor as Mahlodi's own family. Her father was becoming worried that the daughter was getting a little too old to still be unmarried. If she did not take advantage of Phaswa's wealth, marriage would slip through her fingers. It would be humiliating to have a spinster in the family. Because Raditaba's father did not have money he was barred from continuing his love affair with Mahlodi.

That, in itself, would still not have been so bad as to have caused Raditaba to hate Phaswa. As Raditaba and all village men, young and old, were aware, marriage was often snatched away from one man by the luck or daring of another. The women of Tiragalong also shared this line of thinking. They did not refrain from trying to woo or seduce a man simply because he already had a lover. So Phaswa's rather temporary wealth would not have been a problem, were it not for other factors.

Mahlodi, being a woman of remarkable integrity, rejected Phaswa. Even when her father tried to impose his will on her, she remained constant. She remembered well what her father used to tell her, that there were times when there was virtue in stubbornness. But when Raditaba's father could no longer maintain his role in the strained relationship with Mahlodi, he approached the woman who was to become Raditaba's mother.

Phaswa, however, would not leave him in peace. Phaswa's heart told him that the new woman was, indeed, loveable. Even more so than Mahlodi. Phaswa wanted to have a stake in all that was good. He made an effort to follow, once again, in Raditaba's father's tracks. This time, Raditaba's father resolved to declare war on Phaswa. The father was killed in the fight, leaving his new love pregnant.

What Raditaba resented was that when he was born he had no father to take care of him. As a child, his heart would bleed whenever his playmates talked with fondness of the good things their fathers had done for them. And they talked of such things a lot. His mother was too poor to do what some of these fathers did for their children.

Mahlodi, for her part, had to seek another love. She met Refentše's father who, sadly, died shortly after their marriage.

Phaswa came back to her soon after Refentše's funeral, when she was suddenly treated like an outcast. He reminded her that there was always a return to the ruins; it was only to the womb that there could be no return. Since Phaswa seemed to be the only person who showed any interest in her as a full-blooded human being, rather than a scavenging, mysterious, evil spirit, the grudges that she had borne him evaporated like dew in the morning sun.

But, although somewhat of an outcast himself, Phaswa was extremely sensitive to the implications of being associated with her. He suggested that, for a start, their relationship should remain secret while they waited for a lull in the scrutiny of the village. It would not do for Mahlodi to attract further attention to herself, when she was obviously already in a grave position. Phaswa persuaded her that they should only visit each other during the night.

But people also minded their business in the night.

Exactly what it was that Leruo had experienced in his sleep, and even shortly thereafter, was unclear. According to Thabo, when he told the story to his playmates the following day, Leruo had told him many things. Refentše was still alive, he had said. And so was Tshepo. The two lived in one of Mahlodi's dilapidated huts, the very one that was used by Leruo. They only came out in the middle of the night to go to work in Mahlodi's field. They returned before cockcrow, in time to avoid meeting people on their way to the buses that transported them daily to their places of work in Pietersburg. Leruo occasionally heard the two men crying in the night, lamenting their inability to escape the drudgery. When the villagers thought they were burying them, they were in fact merely burying large pieces of wood that were made, through the art of medicines, to resemble them.

It was the kind of news that was so frightening that it could not fail to spread throughout Tiragalong and its neighbourhood in the wink of an eye. When, late in the afternoon, the blowing horn summoned the villagers to the induna's kraal, neighbours also came to share in the disturbing news. In the spirit of Comradeship, the youth from the neighbouring villages came, too.

The meeting was well attended. One could not even spit onto the ground, so thickly was it covered with the presence of angry people.

As usual, one of the most decisive statements was made by Raditaba. He suggested that the younger Comrades should meet separately, for elders were known for being too disruptive at such meetings. In their presence, no decision to punish the witch would be taken quickly enough. Every time a baboon glanced back over its shoulder it slowed its pace, he said, so that its pursuer would catch up with it. They were not going to look back like the foolish baboon.

So the Comrades went their own way, leaving the elders at a loss. The Comrades, when angry, could be callous and fierce. The elders were somewhat afraid of their own children. None of them dared to challenge the Comrades.

Thabo was called to testify to what he had heard. He claimed that Leruo had never said any such thing. Leruo also denied ever seeing the late Refentše and Tshepo in Mahlodi's compound. The Comrades decided to punish Mahlodi all the same. It was understandable that Thabo and Leruo were too frightened to give reliable testimony. It was almost certain that they would not want to give the kind of testimony that might lead to Leruo's aunt's death. But, the fact was that even in their madness, people do not simply scream into the darkness of a rather cold autumn morning, and go running away from the dead, unless the dead are, in fact, still alive. There must have been something of substance to have caused such bizarre behaviour on Leruo's part, the Comrades argued. Surely Refentše and Tshepo must then be still alive? The incident by the graveside had revealed the witch. What Leruo had seen and, in a moment of honesty, without the threat of his aunt's impending death to cow him, confided to his friend Thabo, was just a confirmation of what was already widely known.

As for Phaswa; Raditaba suggested, to much applause, that his secret night meetings with Mahlodi made it painfully clear that he, too, practised the evil art.

Visions Of A Flying Man

he's caught midair
by the corner of an eye
with jacket sleeves & slashes
spread like wings
floating slowly from the twentieth floor
no sound of screaming
fear
is he dead already
or just a man defying death
by refusing to give it the pleasure
of victory
my mind sees
vultures gloating down
to accompany his body
or corpse to the tarred roads
& concrete pavements
of hillbrow
to peck away at this incarnation
of fear of life
fear whose victory lies
in escape
but i hear another voice
haunting me
with searching questions
& worrying misgivings
about my convictions
what if he took a wise decision
it says
& i bow in shame
i bow in shame for the hasty judgement

passed on the floating figure
surrounded by hopeful vultures
& in my shame
i long to know more
of the turbulence
that raged within his heart
& brain
that turbulence whose strength
he could not overcome
& with searing pain
i recall my shattered love
that has pushed me to the verge
of suicide
or perhaps not a shattered love
for the love i still have in abundance
perhaps not a shattered love
but a broken affair
for he who cries
& dies for non existent love
can only be a fool
whose cry is a drum
to whose sonorous songs we dance
but then what of one who dies
for a broken affair
one who cries for the unreachable
or perhaps dies for the mendable
but who knows
who knows
that perhaps it was not really about reaching
or mending
but about something else
a desire to quiet a sore heart
that threatens to swell

within the chest
swell into the skull
& choke the exhausted brain
who am i to judge
the body coming down slowly
at first like a well guided parachute
& as it gathers speed I wonder more
& my thoughts wander once again
towards my broken affair
& my brains retire
with brooding thoughts
of an everlasting
rest

Memories Of Silence

It was not as he had anticipated. Strange that even when he had bulldozed everything out of his way, he should still find life unbearable. Maybe it was to be expected, he mused. Why Lerato had to be the source of this misery he did not quite understand. Should he send her to join her lover in the grave? Or let her live to torment his conscience indefinitely? He was not sure. Not even sure that it was her fault, after all. All she did was call, as she usually did. Except that this time it was not to find out how the day had treated him. She demanded to know why he had influenced the Comrades to necklace her late lover's mother to death, while the real night prowlers were perfectly well known to the two of them.

Sammy stood on the balcony of his two-bedroomed flat in Hillbrow. The balcony faced the street, into which his friend had crushed himself several weeks back. It was not just the thought of Refentše's suicide that was eating away the grey matter in his skull. It was also corroded by his own contribution to the suicide. By the thought of how he had betrayed his friend when Refentše needed him most. As if that was not enough, he then had to betray Refentše's mother as well.

How Lerato came to know about the latter event was still a mystery to Sammy. She refused to say on the telephone. She simply told him that she had just heard of Refentše's mother's gruesome death, and of how Sammy had made it happen. Sammy, who had himself so often condemned beliefs in witchcraft. 'If I were Mandela,' he sometimes said, 'I would re-introduce the death penalty for these Comrades.' He said this even before the old man came to power. On that occasion, he had been speaking his mind to his friend Mogau – Professor – five years before Refentše's suicide. He was, at the time, disgusted with the way the oldest woman in the village had been killed by the Comrades, having been accused of sending the lightning to strike Tshepo. She was said to be jealous that Tshepo had just received sparkling results, in consequence of which his mother was going to have a son who would not just be like the other teachers in Tiragalong. He was going to be a teacher with a degree from the South.

The old woman, Makgolo, had been childless. But since her neighbour had had nothing to do with her childlessness, why she had to begrudge Tshepo's mother remained a mystery to all. Especially since the mother was often the first to assist her whenever she needed help. The village Comrades had very little patience with such ungrateful old witches.

What Sammy hated most on that occasion was his lack of courage to speak up for the old woman. Clearly, no one could prove that she actually was a witch. At the time, Sammy and Refentše were just about to begin their careers as tertiary students. A year before that calamitous afternoon when Tshepo got struck by lightning, their science teacher had looked into the causes of lightning with them. Not because he anticipated that lightning would bring about one of the most devastating disasters in the village a year later, but simply in an attempt to catch up with the syllabus. He had to cover that topic before the arrival of the school inspector. He talked at length about clouds, atmospheric pressure, friction in the air and the subsequent release of energy in the form of lightning. Although he did not lay claim to any science degree or, indeed, a degree of any sort, he seemed knowledgeable enough about what he was teaching. His lesson had confirmed Sammy's doubts about human-sent lightning. So when Tshepo died, Sammy, for one, was prepared to blame his death on nature.

But how could he defend the old woman's case without being accused of practising the art himself? In the end, like a few others who shared his views, he left the soul to depart in its agony. And had lived with an anguished conscience ever since. Yet, when the opportunity presented itself for a second time, he again failed to speak up for what he knew to be the truth.

Refentše had not known that Sammy and Lerato were, in fact, not secret lovers. How could he know, when he had found them together in his bedroom on that fateful day when he went back to pick up his forgotten document at the flat? As far as he was concerned, Sammy must have been constantly biding his time until Refentše left for campus. He would then visit Lerato immediately, for a breakfast of sex. The things wealth can achieve . . . ! The thought rattled in Refentše's skull all day.

Sammy and Lerato could have clarified the issue for him. Except that neither of them was prepared to face Refentše later that day. When Refentše returned from the campus in the afternoon, he found that Lerato had packed her belongings and departed. Later Sammy, too, failed to appear for the scheduled drink. It was the custom for the two friends to enjoy their Friday evening drinks at Refentše's flat while Lerato, who was a good cook, prepared something for them to throw into their stomachs. Sammy, at that time, did not have a lover. And since he had no one to cook for him, kind-hearted Lerato invited him, as Refentše's closest friend, to have supper with them on Fridays and, sometimes, the rest of his weekend meals as well. Initially, Sammy had protested. He knew how to cook for himself, he insisted. It was when Lerato said that the invitation was not about cooking skills, when she pointed out that food was always tastier in the company of friends, that he agreed. That Refentše was happy with the arrangement only went to show that he was a friend, indeed.

It was in such an atmosphere that Lerato and Sammy became very close. Even closer, according to rumour, than any lover should be willing to appreciate. Refentše was warned to be watchful of such closeness by one of his homeboys. 'You never know with people,' the homeboy often said. Refentše was to hear this repeated too frequently. In the end, in a rare moment of impatience, he banished the homeboy from his flat. Not a bad thing, really, for the homeboy, as everyone knew, could not be trusted with any woman. Especially not his friends' wives and girlfriends.

Refentše had a lot of faith in both his lover and friend. Besides, he was not jealous by nature. He was known for letting Sammy and Lerato go off to movies by themselves until late on certain nights, while he stayed behind to prepare his lecture notes.

When Sammy called Refentše to find out whether he had had a good weekend at home after his last visit there, Refentše answered in the affirmative. But that was not, in fact, the case. Refentše disliked people who complained as if they were the only ones with problems. He himself seldom complained. He found it particularly revolting to complain to people about his own family. But a month before, things had been so tough that he had confided to Sammy about the way his mother failed to understand why he was not providing as he should at the homestead. Sammy, the only friend who knew the delicacy of Refentše's situation, offered to give him some money when he next went home.

Refentše declined the offer. Not only did he not want to live on charity, he also preferred not to let his mother believe that he had money when he didn't. After all, that was how she would interpret it. And quite rightly, too. For her son had just been appointed a lecturer.

Refentše had learnt painfully that becoming a lecturer did not necessarily make life easy. The heavy study loans that he had to repay, the equally high rental he had to settle monthly, as well as the notoriously substantial monthly tax deductions and furniture instalments he had to take care of, all these things left him with minimal illusions about the monetary fruits of being a lecturer. He struggled to maintain himself and Lerato, who at that stage was still completing her studies. He admitted to himself that he could not be of much financial use to his mother under such daunting circumstances.

It was on the Thursday before the fateful Friday that Lerato told Sammy, over the telephone, that things were not going well. She complained that Refentše was no longer eating properly. And he kept a sullen silence about what was bothering him. Something, surely, must have gone wrong when he went home the previous weekend.

Sammy guessed what the problem might be. Lerato, he was sure, had no idea that she herself was part of Refentše's problem. According to what Refentše had told him previously, his mother had heard from a reliable cousin that he had a lover in Johannesburg. The mother felt that this lover must be the cause of Refentše's inconsiderate behaviour. Left to himself, the mother was certain, Refentše was, by nature, very caring, and she would not have to endure this kind of suffering from her son, given the fact that he was now working. It must therefore be the bitch's fault! After all, Jo'burg women were known by the people of Tiragalong to be bloodsuckers.

The worst thing was that the cousin had also intimated that the woman concerned came from Hillbrow. Although Refentše's mother had never been to Johannesburg herself, she had heard a lot of disgusting stories about Hillbrow. Theft. Murder. Prostitution . . . Could it be that her son's sense of morality had deteriorated? Could he have stooped so low that he would even run after prostitutes? When she said to Refentše, 'You leave her, or you are no longer my son!' she thought that she was protecting her son from the fierce storms of life. In her grief and wrath, she forgot to listen to her son's side of things.

Sammy knew all this. He also knew that it would soon be necessary to take Lerato into their confidence on the issue. Refentše's protective attitude, which accounted for his reluctance to reveal the truth to her, was understandable. Yet, Sammy reasoned with himself, it was unfair that she should have the burden of looking after Refentše, absorbing his pain and depression, when she did not have so much as an inkling as to the source of these fountains. Lerato was reasonable, Sammy thought. A better knowledge of the root cause of her lover's problems might help her, and everyone concerned, to help Refentše. It was in this spirit of hopefulness that Sammy made an appointment to see Lerato at the earliest possible time.

Lerato was still in bed when Sammy arrived the next morning. It was very early, just after Refentše's departure for work. The knowledge of Refentše's unhappiness weighed her spirits down. She was still brooding on this subject when a knock shook her abruptly into remembering that she should be up already. For Sammy had said that he would come by early this morning.

She jumped quickly out of bed. In her gratitude at Sammy's arrival, she forgot that she wasn't properly dressed and opened the door for him in her night attire. Sammy was later unsure whether it was the attractiveness of her bare thighs that stirred the well of emotion in his heart and his manhood. Every time he tried to rebuild the memory of their encounter, all he could achieve was the remembrance of the strange, sudden realisation that he had never really appreciated the full beauty of Lerato's looks before. He remembered, too, that the boy in his pants had suddenly, almost unaccountably, become restless. He found himself visualising Lerato's breasts, which now stood erect in her rather transparent nightdress, cupped in Refentše's gentle hands as his friend poured words of sweetness into her ears . . . Lerato replying with deep kisses, and their words melting into each other's mouths . . . In this bliss of his imagination, he substituted himself for Refentše.

Sammy never was able to justify his unpremeditated conduct that morning. Not even to himself. It was perhaps this failure that gnawed away at his conscience. He also wondered why Lerato had not objected. Not even slightly. She had let him embrace her tenderly. And then kiss her full on the mouth. Lerato, the devout lover of Refentše. Lerato the strong one who had overcome the temptation of better men than he . . . Sammy could not understand it.

After their fleeting bliss, which Refentše's unexpected arrival had shattered, the new couple did not quite know what to say to each other. It was heavy and oppressive, the silence that lay between them. So heavy that Sammy left as soon as he could. It remained for Lerato alone to try and settle issues with her lover.

Since his flat was only five floors up from street level, Sammy could, conceivably, have witnessed his friend in the air, on his way down to his crushing end in the street. But he did not remain in his flat that day. From Refentše's place, he went back to his own, took his bank card, and left. He found that the atmosphere in his place caused him untold claustrophobia. He wanted to open windows for fresh air before going out. Then he discovered that there was nothing to open, since he had already opened them before he left earlier for Refentše's flat. Thinking that the air outside might help to clear his thinking, he directed the heavy soles of his shoes onto the Hillbrow pavements.

There was no fresh air to be found in the streets, either. Incidents of physical violence in Quartz Street, which he witnessed, only sank him deeper into the horror of what he had done. Nor was his claustrophobia relieved by the usual invitations from prostitutes who made it their business to display their wares in the street.

I am not a rapist . . .

He suffered visions of police stopping him in the street, humiliating him before every one. He found himself starting nervously when they suddenly appeared, bent on some unknown mission of their own.

I'm not a rapist . . . The persistent echo reverberated at the back of his mind.

His thoughts continued to transform, into loud, hysterical voices thrown into the streets of Hillbrow, hitting helplessly against the mighty concrete and brick walls of the tall buildings, only to return as echoes come to haunt his soul.

I am not a rapist . . .

Sammy walked into his favourite pub. But he found he could not drink anything. He did not even taste the beer he had paid for. He wondered whether to go back to Lerato. Could he lay his soul bare to her, and apologise? He faltered, as he had so often done before. He would wait until Refentše was back from work and apologise to him instead. No sooner had he decided that, however, than he found that every tick of his wristwatch gradually eroded the conviction that Refentše would listen with understanding. It increasingly became doubtful whether his friend would listen at all.

Lerato, too, did not quite know what to do. Initially, she thought she would wait for Refentše to come back in the afternoon, and explain to him. But she soon hesitated. Would Refentše understand? It would be almost impossible to convince him that what had happened could not be helped. At least, she could not help it. Or, could she?

Her memory recounted her deep thankfulness upon Sammy's arrival, her strong desire to kiss him in gratitude. And, when Sammy initiated . . . Could she really not help it? And what did one make of Refentše's mute behaviour in the face of that dreadful encounter? For the first time since her love life with Refentše started, she began to fear him. She packed her things.

She found she could not talk about the incident. Not even to her mother, with whom she had always discussed the most intimate problems. Her mother's prejudice in favour of Refentše was well known to her. An ideal son-in-law, she had said a number of times. Lerato winced at the thought of her mother's likely reaction, were she to discover the roots of her daughter's misery. She winced, and her silence was cemented.

When the mother arrived home later that evening from work and found her darling daughter crying inconsolably, and learnt that her lover had committed suicide, she said to herself that there could be no better reason for crying. The mother's ill-informed condolences did not make Lerato's silence a more bearable load to carry.

Neither did things improve when Lerato received a call several weeks later. Sammy had encouraged the Comrades of Tiragalong to necklace Refentše's mother, the caller had announced. The mother was accused of practising witchcraft, of having bewitched Refentše and a few other villagers. She had been known, ever since Refentše's funeral, to be a witch. This fact was revealed on that hot Saturday morning, when she fell into her son's grave as she was throwing a handful of soil into it. It was unheard of for anyone to fall into an open grave without good reason. Medicine-men had established long ago that it was only when the witch had killed the deceased that such bizarre conduct could result. It was said to be some kind of punishment from the deceased one's Ancestors.

According to the caller, it was Refentše's youngest cousin who had revealed to his friend that Refentše's mother was, indeed, a witch. Tshepo and Refentše were still alive. They remained shut inside one of Refentše's mother's huts during the day, only allowed out at midnight when all people were asleep. She employed them to do the hard chores in her field. The village, unknowingly, had buried two logs of wood that were made through medicines to resemble the two deceased.

The boy, Thabo, had passed on to his friends this frightening news that his friend, Refentše's youngest cousin, had told him under an oath of secrecy. His friends, under the same oath, told their friends, who in turn told their friends . . . News is like smoke, it spreads. With the speed of lightning, all the village and its neighbourhood learnt that what had been revealed at Refentše's funeral was confirmed by the child, Leruo, who had come to stay with Refentše's mother soon after her son's suicide. Whose evidence could be more reliable than an insider's? the Comrades demanded.

Nobody had cared to find out how the child had discovered such a costly truth.

It still might have been fine if Refentše's mother had only bewitched her own son. But her bewitching of Tshepo as well had made her case particularly ugly. Especially because the Comrades were misled into believing that it was another old woman who had sent the lightning to strike Tshepo.

One Comrade had pointed out that all the youth of Tiragalong were potential victims of Refentše's mother's whims, if they should let her live. All the youth, he had emphasised, especially the ones who intended to study at a university. Must they then continue to accuse and kill unlucky, defenceless people like the other old woman, while the true masters and mistresses of witchcraft roamed freely as if they owned the world? It was surely up to the Comrades to clear the ground on which they were going to play, and thorns like Refentše's mother must be set on fire.

It was Sammy, the caller told Lerato, who then spoke at length about how the death of Refentše – whose voluntary services to the village, especially his teaching and library work at the village school, were well known – was like the death of the advancement of the village. Yes, death, Sammy had insisted. For was it not the same as death when one was locked up in a night prowler's hut, being of service to no one? Unlike the other Comrades, he spoke as Refentše's closest friend, who had intimate insight into the kind of vision that Refentše had had for the welfare of Tiragalong. With his oratory skills, Sammy could not fail to touch the very bottom of his fellow Comrades' hearts. It was by this eloquence that they were moved to action, the caller concluded to Lerato.

This time Lerato could not keep quiet. Her unhappiness at her and Sammy's roles in Refentše's suicide had already begun urging her to end her own life. On numerous occasions she had asked herself what she had to live for. Sammy's further betrayal of Refentše's family did not make the vicious question any more bearable. Lerato picked up the receiver only minutes after the disturbing call had ended, and dialled Sammy's number.

'Sammy,' she had said with calm gravity, 'Sammy – so it was not enough to kill your friend?'

Yes, Sammy thought to himself, Lerato is dangerous.

Sammy had not intended to have to witness Refentše's mother burn to death. Indeed, the sight of her with huge tyres, wet with petrol, stacked around her neck had haunted him ever since. There were times when he thought he could still hear the shrill screams issuing from her burning hut, in which she had been locked. The vividly remembered smell, too, assaulted his nostrils as though it were not just a memory. The smell of roasted human flesh, as his friend Mogau had once phrased it. Roasted human flesh . . .

He had thought that the accusation levelled against Refentše's mother, and her subsequent death, would discourage any probing into the actual fountains of Refentše's suicide. Sammy was simply preventing his own demise, for the Comrades were keen on avenging the unfair death of Refentše. Now, Lerato's words made it clear that the issue of Refentše's suicide would be pursued once more, sooner or later. Most probably sooner.

The thought of sending Lerato to join her lover in the grave sent a cold feeling down Sammy's spine. He shivered. Or should he rather let her live, and himself commit suicide instead? Although Sammy would not necessarily have to jump from the balcony of his flat, since there were so many better ways of dying, the thought of suicide inevitably brought back images of Refentše's disfigured corpse. Again, Sammy shivered . . .

The Menacing Lights

Even before Liz could jump out of the minibus taxi that she had caught from her place of work in the city, she could see that all the lights in her house were out. She found it quite strange. Her daughter, Lerato, was not the kind of person who would ordinarily go to bed before nine in the evening. She was a devout reader, and in the event of having nothing to read, or when she simply felt lazy, Lerato would spend hours on end playing her CDs and cassettes. Liz, who did not really have much time for music, could not help getting used to listening to Stimela's *See the world through the eyes of a child*. Lerato played the song constantly. It reminded her of Refentše, her lover who used to love the song, and who had committed suicide on discovering that she had become lovers with their mutual friend.

Unlike Lerato, Liz did not know the reason for the suicide. And there was nothing tangible to allow her to guess wisely. To her, the song was a touching expression of Lerato's memory of her joyful days with her late lover in their flat in Hillbrow.

In time the song came to mean a little more to Liz. She was soon to associate it with the melancholy look that settled unambiguously, and remained for a bit too long, on Lerato's face. Every time this song played, Liz could visualise the deteriorating spark of youth in her daughter's looks, the youth that was gnawed away at by grief. She noticed with consternation that Lerato was becoming increasingly less talkative, and beginning to adopt a mood of severely haunted brooding.

But Liz never really knew why Lerato was responding in such a self-destructive manner to Refentše's death. Once or twice she had tried to discuss it with Lerato. Her daughter's reply was unexpected. They were used to discussing in detail Lerato's problems, including those that had to do with matters of the heart. This time all Lerato offered was that she would try to overcome her grief and be herself once more. She also wondered aloud why, if Refentše had had severe problems, he did not at least hint at them, if not discuss them with her.

Liz persuaded herself that Lerato felt betrayed. Now, whether or not someone had committed suicide, betrayal in itself was enough to cause resentment, Liz thought. But what could it lead to when death was also involved?

It was clear, since the lights were off, that this evening Lerato was not engaged in any reading. It was also unlikely that she was on an outing somewhere. She rarely went out in the evenings. As a young girl, Liz used to discourage her from such activities. Alexandra, she had pointed out to her daughter, was full of vultures. Robbers. Murderers. Rapists . . . Any instance of careless living could easily lead one into trouble. Lerato was to hear these words echoed with varying degrees of intensity by her mother's friends and other grown-ups. But her real understanding of the truth of their words dawned when she was in her second year at the university, and came to haunt her with a persistent, piercing sharpness.

One morning she received an upsetting call. A mutual friend of theirs had been gang-raped at gunpoint in an ordeal that involved car hijacking, the caller said. The friend herself was later to relate in person to Lerato the most haunting description of the incident. Just as disturbing as the act itself, was the persistent feeling of uncleanness that the friend now suffered, so that she could not, after the event, establish any normal love relationship with a man. She spoke with halting words that failed to express her frustration adequately and with eyes brimming with tears that found their way down her wasted cheeks, and further down, to her chin, from where they dropped onto and were absorbed by the carpet.

For the first time in their long friendship Lerato could find no soothing words to say to her friend. Since then, Lerato had gone to great lengths to steer clear of obviously dangerous routes – even more so after she herself was caught in a similar robbery ordeal. Though in her case, fortunately, without having to taste the bitter fruit of rape.

She was to share these tales with her mother quite often. And, knowing her daughter as she did, Liz now assumed that Lerato must have simply decided to take her rest earlier than usual. Liz was later brought to wonder why, everything considered, she had allowed herself to carry Lerato into this world at all, only for it to reach this end – to be tormented infinitely by the sight of her daughter at this unnatural rest – when other women committed abortion in the face of their major misgivings.

To say that Liz had had doses of disappointment in her life is also partly to tell the story of one of the sons of Tiragalong. Although the villagers liked to believe that they were in many ways better than Johannesburgers, those who were acquainted with Tiragalong's deeds while in Jo'burg had alternative stories to tell. One such story concerns Lerato's father.

Liz and Piet met when they both arrived in Jo'burg for the first time, four or five years before Lerato was born. Liz came to try life in the city when, after her matriculation, Durban failed to provide work for her. A similar situation applied to Piet. With his matric certificate, he could at least have worked as a clerk in a store in Pietersburg. But he was unfortunate not to find employment. It was when his newly married wife fell pregnant that Piet resolved to go in search of greener pastures in the city. It was painfully clear that hard times lay ahead for their family. The limited livestock that his parents had left them had died of hoof-and-mouth disease the year before. He simply had to devise other ways of supporting his family.

But for both Liz and Piet things were not easy in the city. After an exhausting search for decent jobs, with several interruptions due to imprisonment under the Pass Law system, Piet had thought of returning to Tiragalong. It was the news of the birth of their son that persuaded him to resume his search. He remembered the saying in Tiragalong that the person in search of a queen bee needed to dig very deep, right into the bowels of the earth, in order to be successful. Queen bees were known to make remarkable ingredients in various forms of medicine, and doctors who could access them would have powers of healing – together with the wealth that goes with such powers – far superior to their competitors. In his case, Piet was preoccupied with questions of simple survival. But he also knew that survival could be elusive. Especially if you were too ready to sit on your hands, while other people used their buttocks for the purpose.

Much against his will, then, he ended up accepting the job of gardener in Honeydew. It was there that he and Liz met.

Piet's employers had just dismissed their cook, who had lost patience with their mischievous child. They themselves did not really spare the rod as far as this child was concerned. But, at the same time, they did not allow their cook, or any of their domestic servants, to spank their children. They felt so strongly about the matter that they asked Piet to find them someone to replace the cook, who had transgressed this rule, with immediate assumption of duty.

At the time, Liz had come to visit her cousin next door for the weekend. Although Piet had not been working there long, he was already getting along well with his black neighbours in the suburb. It was important to get along well. As everyone knew, when your house caught fire it was neighbours, and not relatives, who arrived first to help extinguish it. It was best of all, of course, when the neighbours were also relatives. In this case they were not. Now there was the fire. Piet shouted for help. The neighbours listened attentively to the call. Liz was the water with which the fire was extinguished.

The only thing left for Piet, his neighbours and Liz, was to sort out her transport difficulties. It would have been too costly for Liz to travel all the way from Alexandra every day for six days a week, especially since she had not been earning thus far. She spent the first week of her new job with her cousin. Which is to say that she lived in hiding. Her cousin's employers had no problem with visitors. But they did mind extra residents in their yard. Water and electricity charges were high, was their constant reminder to their employees.

It was Piet who suggested the fateful move that led to the breaking of Liz's heart, years later, when he went to join his Ancestors in the underworld.

'Liz, how long is this going to go on?'

'What do you mean?'

'I mean . . . Why don't you move in here with me? The boss said I could bring my wife to come and stay with me. But you know how expensive it would be to bring her here. Besides, someone has to take care of the homestead.'

Liz had listened with astonishment. She wondered what went on in the minds of men. For Piet was the umpteenth man to issue such an invitation to her since her arrival in the city, several months back. She discussed her worries with her cousin. It seemed to her that it was going to be difficult working with a man who had helped her, and who, unexpectedly, seemed to have had a hidden motive all along.

'Cousy,' the cousin had replied. 'I don't know what you want me to say. But that is how we live in Jo'burg. How do you think I get the money to send to my children at home? Either you get someone to help you, or your children will be forced to shit water while their friends eat well and know what they are carrying with them when they go to the toilet. I've been hiding this from you and everyone at home. People at home like to pretend that life is about morals. They make it impossible for those who find it difficult here to tell them painful truths. So I could not tell them much about how I have been coping all along. But I will tell you, since you want to hear. I have three partners now. They all know each other. I tell them to come only at agreed times. If you're lucky, they co-operate. If they are wooden-headed you find yourself in a toilet pit. This is Jo'burg for you, Cousy!'

Liz spent the night thinking hard. She was shocked that her cousin, a model of good conduct, should tell her this. When she went back to Alexandra for the weekend, she asked her other close relatives who had been working in the city for some time about such issues. Only a few criticised such behaviour, although it turned out later that some of the severest critics of immorality were just as immoral as the targets of their criticism. Others said it was up to her to make up her own mind. She was a woman now, they said. But none offered to reassure her that she could change life for the better. One went so far as to hint that if Piet were to be thoroughly disgusted with her, Liz could very easily lose her new job. All he would need to do was say to her bosses that he had made a mistake, and that he had found a better and more dependable cook.

In the end, though, it was not this threat that decided Liz. Nor did she intend to emulate her cousin with an endless string of lovers. No! Liz had reasons of her own for agreeing. It did not take her long to decide that Piet was, in fact, a good man. After working with him for a few weeks and observing his conduct towards her, she persuaded herself that he was not motivated, in securing her the job, by selfish motives. A man with a generosity of spirit, in this city where almost everyone appeared to sneer at morality, was difficult to meet. And since she was single, it would not problematise her relationships in any way.

That Piet was married with a child was none of her business, really. What his wife saw in him was what Liz thought she could see herself. A good lover, so she had learnt since she was very young, had to be snatched away from other people who recognised the same qualities in him or her as you yourself did. It was, in fact, with the hope of securing a good marriage for herself that she bravely said to Piet, who was already giving up on the possibility of having a relationship with this Durban woman: 'I have been thinking about it, Piet.'

'Thinking about what?' asked Piet, who half imagined that Liz was referring to what could have led to the sudden death of their bosses' beloved dog. On account of which the two had been subjected to close questioning and cross-questioning.

'What you said to me the other day. About coming to live with you.'

Piet nodded slightly. He was sure, even after the few weeks that they had worked together, that Liz's integrity was not in question. He knew her answer could only be a definite 'No!'

He had to wait patiently for a moment while Liz seemed to pay great attention to the coffee that was brewing on the stove. Then, just when it seemed she would resume speaking, the telephone rang and she dashed across the room to answer the call.

'They are going to eat out. They will only come home after ten.'

Piet found it torturous, trying to disguise his interest in their earlier subject. A tentative shimmer of hope, emerging during the period of waiting, struggled in the iron grip of giant pessimism in his chest. He had more important things to worry about, he found, than to be bothered about when the bosses were returning. Just so long as they returned in good time to pay him and Liz at the end of the month!

'You were saying . . . '

'Ah yes! I forget. I was saying that I have thought about the issue. I will live with you if you are still interested. The only thing I would hate is to see you following every skirt that you see around. As long as we support each other, and you remember your family at home, we can live happily together.'

Piet half opened his mouth in amazement. It was not just on account of the joy he felt at the prospect of living with Liz, whom he had begun to love already. He was also amazed that she could spare thought for his family in Tiragalong in her plans.

But, simultaneously, a glitter of disappointment showed its face to his heart as soon as Liz broke this happy news. For what partly made her lovable to him, he began to realise there and then, was that she had seemed intent, at first at least, on maintaining some veneer of integrity.

The two scraped a living together for several years. Nothing was easy. But they could not really be counted among the saddest couples in Jo'burg. Thus it was that Liz was quite grieved when, one Sunday evening, their employers brought her news to the effect that Piet had been stabbed to death, for as yet unknown reasons, in Alexandra. The police officer who telephoned the employers said, as the police always said, that investigations were already underway.

Although still unbeknown to Piet's wife that she had been sharing her husband with a 'Johannesburger', she and Liz now shared equally in the grief. It could not even be said with any certainty that so-and-so felt the pain a little more. Suffice to say that Liz's cousin could not understand the depth of her pain over the death of this country bumpkin. There were so many other men of real worth, in Honeydew, not to mention the rest of the city, she suggested.

Unable to face working in that same yard without Piet and finding her cousin's cynicism towards relationships much more severe than she could at that moment bear, Liz was soon to leave and seek work elsewhere. The timing was right, as it happened. For Hillbrow Hospital needed people with matric to fill several new posts in the lower rungs of its administration.

Even then, Liz's tormented memory kept on revisiting Honeydew. Like Piet's wife in Tiragalong, Liz, too, was to think deeply about the implications of Piet's death for her child. For she was in the early stages of her pregnancy when he died. In her view, she was not really ready to have a child. But she thought about Piet with deepening passion and sadness every time the notion of abortion flashed across her mind. Even with her apprehension about the future, she found that there was still something satisfying about carrying their child. In the end, she resolved to simply let live.

Left to her own meagre income, bringing up Lerato and, in due course, her younger sister, in Alexandra – and partly helping to support her extended family in her village near Durban – Liz did not find living an easy task at all.

Now, as she unlocked the door to the house, Liz was wondering how her daughter could ever hope to fall asleep with music playing so loudly. Walking into her daughter's room and switching on the lights, Liz was reminded, in that single frozen instant of discovery, of her long sufferings and her initial troubled contemplations of abortion. Lerato's face had, even in the final moments, managed to maintain its look of haunted brooding. Poisonous tablets lay carelessly scattered on the CD player. And Liz could find no clue to the possible cause of her daughter's suicide.

The words *See the world* . . . were brought to an abrupt halt as she switched off the CD player, without bothering to delete the REPEAT command first. But the song did not cease to reverberate in her mind, long after those first moments of discovery.

Interlude: Oasis

oasis
a place of joy
& entertainment where hearts wake up
blink
open their eyes
to the frailty of their pleasure
it is tiragalong nightmaring
about hillbrow sluts
bodies leaning against walls
& hymens breaking as the village migrant drops seeds
just by the concrete pavements
babies sprout like mushrooms
after soaking drizzles
& the heartrending screams of the little ones
yell after the elusive father
while the village wife
plants sweet kisses onto the concubine's lipstick
residues on sweetie's lips
with visions of a brighter tomorrow glowing
in her soft gaze
she swallows hard
smacks her lips
the migrant
returns home later to watch
communality in action
not pictures on the big screen
or cruel images piercing through these pages
it is fellow villagers populating his hut
with new mouths
that gape with horror at dad's bigholed trouser pockets

remembering the lost seeds
now roaming hillbrow streets
he sits there elbows digging into the table the chin cupped
within his hands
brooding because he can't breed
or having bred flesh of suffering
now stalking hillbrow streets having bred like a rabbit
now he can only breed
venomous thoughts
thoughts like scorpions with raised tails
ready to strike
while the wife
& the concubine slit each other's throats
from within his palpitating heart
scrambling for sweetie's tattered attention
that attends the wailing song of the cricket
hidden under the bed
lovers sandwiched between the bones
of their hearts moaning for attention
& blood knotting chains of communality
& hillbrow quickies pulsating
through unsettled memories
ensnared hearts bleed
& drown in torrents of blood
jutting out glaring wounds
learning outcomes of a meeting
as tarmac & flesh
crash in head-on collision
one pulled to the stars
& the other to the ground
from a flat balcony
gravity
newton looks on with soaring consternation

while corpses float in oceans of blood
red tears bathe the sadness sounded
by the blowing horn
new love drowned by memories of silence
over the fountains of tears
or overwhelmed by the knowing warnings
of worldwise lovers erecting shattered mirrors
with tales of woe
for new love to piece together
if it dares
the refractions that pop out of the glasses
& leap into the mirrors
of bursting hearts
it is what you read on a toilet wall in the basement
in senate house
an accompaniment to the bodiless genitalia
minding their business
on / against the wall
& the wits painter painting in vain
as the toilet artist strikes
again

Shades Of Sanctuary

Terror put the handset back. He leaned against the telephone booth, not making way for the people behind him to make their calls. He looked around with bloodshot eyes, as if to dare anyone to protest. He was pleased with himself. He recalled with pleasure Lerato's distress on the phone. Who did she think she was? he thought, as he felt in his pocket for the packet of dagga.

Presently, he remembered that the people were there, like him, to make use of Telkom's services. He moved aside to give them space.

It would not have been such a pleasure to torment Lerato had her lover not treated him like shit. It began one day when Terror gave Refentše his opinion about the closeness between Lerato and Sammy. Refentše and Sammy might be the best of friends, but Terror could not trust any woman with a friend. Or maybe any man with a lover of his. He did not quite remember how he had phrased it to Refentše. But that did not really matter. What did matter was that Refentše – the fool! – had taken offence at a fellow villager's manly advice.

The impact of this advice did not show on Refentše until Terror had repeated it a number of times. Terror only became aware of this when Refentše made his move to banish him from the flat. With his characteristically frank approach, Refentše had told Terror that it was he, Terror, who could not be trusted with his friends' women. In Refentše's case it was even worse. For, Refentše had explained, he and Terror were not even friends. They were merely fellow villagers who happened to live close to each other in Hillbrow, and to help each other out now and then.

Refentše did not go into so much detail as to point out to Terror that Terror, in fact, never returned the hospitality that he received unfailingly. But one issue was worth mentioning: Refentše mentioned it, and its mention left Terror filled with cold contempt for his fellow villager.

That was not all. Terror was also reminded of an incident from his and Refentše's school days.

One fine Friday morning Terror had woken up in a mood for hunting. He decided to go hunting by himself while other village youths went to school. The following Monday, when their class teacher wanted to punish him with the thick stick that was always lying prominently on the table, Terror had protested. He bravely told the teacher that corporal punishment was illegal – which was not the case, then – and that, even though he admitted his faults, he could not allow anyone, including the school principal, to treat him like a worthless dog.

It was during the lunchbreak that Terror announced to his classmates that he had a thing or two to discuss with them. None of them went out to lunch that day. Not that they did not want to. But Terror was ruthless, and any act of defiance of his words might have led to a battering for the deviant. There were just a few, like Refentše, who did not fear him at all. Even they stayed, though, just to hear what Terror had to say to them.

What Terror told the class was hardly a significant revelation. Most had expected that he would complain about the class teacher. Some had even gone so far as to expect that he would call for a formal complaint against him, through the head prefects, to the principal.

But what he suggested shook the class. None of them had dreamt of a strike in the school. Tiragalong High was very peaceful. Now, how did one begin to launch a strike? As if to rub salt into the already smarting wound, Terror further said that what the staff needed to bring them to their senses, was a genuinely violent action. He had been to Johannesburg, he said. He had learnt a few things when Black Power was raging through the townships of the city, when students protested against the imposition of Afrikaans as the only medium of instruction in their schools. In the end, with much bloodshed, he said, the government was persuaded to listen to the children.

For many of the pupils, Black Power was a vague term that they recalled hearing on the radio during the late 1970s. Migrants from the city had also come bringing gory stories of strikes and protests in the

South at the time. Most of Terror's classmates had just begun school, then. They could not be expected to have understood much of what was happening at the time. Even had they not been too young, Black Power would most likely have denoted something quite negative to them. For the radio always referred to the upheavals of the period as being influenced by terrorists who did not only want to render the country ungovernable, but also did not have the well-being of black children at heart.

Unlike his classmates, Terror was older. He was in the same class as they were simply because he had failed on numerous occasions, in addition to having dropped out of school several times. Armed with his more mature understanding of politics, plus the added advantage of having been in the South when the political struggle was raging like an angry fire that was blown into even greater anger by zealous winds, he had hoped to persuade his classmates, and with their support the whole school, that the school administration was cruel and inconsiderate of the needs of the pupils.

Most people were undecided about his suggestions. Corporal punishment did them no good, they all agreed. There was a need to complain against it, they agreed again. But most thought that Refentše, their class prefect, who was also one of the head prefects of the school, should go with the other head prefect to present their complaints to the staff and the principal. The idea of bloodshed did not appeal to them. Most of them liked their good, hard-working teachers, anyway.

It was chiefly Refentše who dealt Terror's objectives the most severe blow. 'Let us recall the situation,' he had said to the class. 'Terror did not come to school on Friday. He was not sick. At least he admitted this to the teacher. I think that Terror must take his punishment the way we all do, while we are busy making our representation to the administration. Who is he to be an exception? Why should we attack our teachers, and possibly damage our school, just because Terror has been punished? When a baboon throws a challenge, you can be sure that its cave is close by. It knows it has sanctuary in the cave. Terror knows where his sanctuary is.

Ladies and gentlemen,' he concluded, assuming a mock-official tone, 'if you are his sanctuary, I wish you good luck in your role.'

As he sat down, another fearless classmate stood up.

'Refentše speaks very well, indeed,' he said, looking gravely into his classmates' eyes. 'These are hard times for us. We will be writing in three weeks time. Those who aim to fail can follow Terror. I hope the hares and hedgehogs that you will kill in your hunting will secure you a healthy future.'

Terror had stared at Refentše dangerously while he was speaking. Now he shifted his glare towards the last speaker, who was rather amused by Terror's look. Terror knew that his plan had failed. Refentše was usually a dangerous opponent. Not because he was malicious, but simply because he spoke his mind fearlessly. And his mind was often clear about what he had to lose and gain in any venture. Moreover, because of his sincerity, Refentše always had great support from the school as a whole.

And the other speaker . . . the bastard! He, too, was highly regarded.

Terror could only hope that Sammy would not now stand up to talk in his turn. The trio usually made a formidable front. If Sammy, too, spoke up, Terror knew that the whole school would turn against him. He prayed to the powers-that-were to spare him that humiliation.

Sammy, however, remained seated, too busy quietly brooding over his own personal problems to pay attention to Terror's garbage. Even so, Terror did not, on that occasion, receive the support that he had hoped for. He hated Refentše and his supporters from that day on. And he also had to hate Sammy, for his silence. If Sammy had only supported him, things might have turned out very differently. Terror believed that Sammy had kept quiet simply because he did not want to oppose his friend, Refentše, in front of so many eyes. Coward! Terror felt that Sammy deserved as much contempt as was due to Refentše. For in Terror's mind, there was no doubt that Sammy had contributed equally to his failure to spark a revolt in the school.

When Refentše confronted Terror in his flat in Hillbrow, it woke bitter reminders of that earlier incident of humiliating failure. He resolved to take his revenge when he had the chance.

It took the occurrence of Sammy's madness to reveal the truth about what had led to Refentše's suicide. Whether it was his own betrayal of Refentše gnawing at his conscience, or the raving witchcraft in the village that had led to his unhinged state, was a cause for much gossip. What everyone knew for sure was that Sammy had one day turned up in Tiragalong with all his belongings, swearing that there was no joy to be found in the city. He talked wildly about the face of the late Refentše that followed him everywhere – to work, to the bars, to soccer matches . . .

'It's not me, Refentše!' he would occasionally scream, to the villagers' alarm.

In a somewhat broken speech, Sammy gave the village to understand that he and Lerato had, together, betrayed Refentše. It was a revelation that got the village Comrades to thinking quite seriously about things. For they had previously concluded that Refentše was bewitched by his own mother, who put into him the thought of committing suicide. The mother was also rumoured to have bewitched a few other villagers. It was particularly the latter point that left the Comrades with no other choice except to make a braai of her and her secret lover, who was believed to practise the evil art with her.

Sammy himself had encouraged the Comrades to roast her alive, hoping that her distracting death would prevent any rigorous enquiries into the death of his friend. Such enquiries would have inevitably revealed that Refentše had jumped from the balcony of his flat straight into the street, twenty levels down, because of grief at discovering what his lover and friend had been up to.

For this revelation, the Comrades would have taken Sammy severely to task. He knew well enough that they were quite keen to avenge Refentše's death. They saw it as a grave loss for the whole village. For Refentše was not only one of the finest young men in the village as far as character and conduct was concerned. He was also the most highly educated. Before he died, he had just begun to teach at the university in Johannesburg. And although he did not see it in that light himself, the villagers believed that his education was going to benefit them in numerous ways. Most of them saw his demise as the death of their envisaged advancement.

When Refentše's mother was killed, Terror, who had been greatly amazed at Sammy's touching and persuasive speech in favour of her death, had immediately phoned Lerato to inform her how Refentše's friend had contributed towards his mother's murder.

Lerato did not understand the village politics. She only knew that Sammy could not be expected to encourage the village to follow the right trails, since that would expose the way in which he had, in effect, killed his friend. Her understanding did not mean that she agreed with his actions. She still loved Refentše very much, and her regret at what she and Sammy had done was profound.

When she phoned Sammy to reproach him for his conduct, Sammy was seriously discomforted by her reproach.

What disturbed him most was his fear that Lerato was so disgusted about the mother's unwarranted death that she was well on her way to revealing the truth about the real cause of Refentše's death. That would be a very dangerous disclosure. For Sammy at least. He even, at one point, toyed with the idea of killing Lerato in order to cover up his trail once more. But the prospect of killing her rested uneasily on his already haunted conscience.

He then contemplated his own suicide but, again, faltered.

The burden of what he had done continued to weigh heavily on him. Each time he tried to sleep he saw Refentše's face with its customary gentle smile. Or he remembered vividly the crushed corpse face of his late friend. Just as often, he would have visions of the smile and the corpse merging into a new and terrible shape.

Then, as he tried to retreat from Refentše's many faces, he would imagine himself plunging into the huge flames in the hut from which Refentše's mother's shrill screams emanated. The flames leapt out into the open air and voraciously lapped at the otherwise cool breeze, so that, although Sammy managed to pull his friend's mother out of the hut, they both remained ensnared in the hot lairs of the Comrades' wrath. At such moments Sammy would remember Lerato's calm but grave reproach.

'Sammy,' she had said, 'Sammy, so it was not enough to kill your friend?'

Sammy's colleagues wondered greatly at his changed behaviour at work. He would shrug and scream unexpectedly, then just as swiftly remember that he must keep his secret. With a heavy heart he would return to his work, only to be tormented by Refentše's faces appearing on his computer screen.

He decided to leave his work and concentrate on his own business. But the hallucinations followed him everywhere. His torment was not eased by the sound of Refentše's mother's screams popping out of the concrete walls of Hillbrow skyscrapers, transforming into echoes that reverberated persistently within his skull.

It was with the hope of visiting a herbalist that he went home to Tiragalong. Herbalists were said to have powers to restore peace to a tormented soul. Sammy did not really believe in traditional doctors. But he had reached the point at which, when pursued ones became desperate, it was not uncommon to see them throwing feathers at their pursuers, seemingly with the hope that the feathers would somehow change into stones.

The greatest herbalist in the village, after consulting his bones, accused Sammy of playing dangerous games with him. How could Sammy hope to receive any help from him when he knew exactly what was wrong with him? the herbalist demanded. Sammy cringed in the face of his towering wrath.

'Do I look like a murderer?' he shouted, much to Sammy's alarm, since he had not expected such accusatory questions, clothed in such sarcastic tones. 'The Gods are angry! You have killed innocent souls. I do not wish to gather the hot embers of the Gods' wrath onto my own skull. Go away from my yard before I . . . !'

Overwhelmed by the depth of feeling in the possessed one's words, Sammy speedily found his way into the dark streets of Tiragalong.

His despair drummed triumphantly within his heart and head, until it threatened to disjoin the very components of his skull. With the doctor's relentlessly cruel tones reverberating in his brain, Sammy saw afresh the hideousness of his cowardly actions. His hallucinatory visions of Refentše's faces and the rapidly increasing shrillness of his mother's screams mingled with the booming voice of the doctor, until the three phenomena became one. Every now and then, the computer screens from work would flash rapidly and incomprehensibly across his eyes, in the pitch-black darkness of the Tiragalong streets.

Sammy's dire attempts to calm his deeply confused thoughts did not bear any positive fruit. It was out of his fast-deteriorating powers of reasoning that he talked about Refentše's suicide, and his own contribution towards it.

The Comrades met once more to discuss the problem of witchcraft in the village. It was a dispirited meeting. Every one of them could read the heaviness of feeling in the rest. It was now clear that Refentše's mother could not have been a witch. It was similar to the time they had discovered that the old woman, Makgolo, whom they had necklaced to death for having sent lightning to strike their fellow youth, Tshepo, was not a witch after all. On that day it had seemed painfully clear that it was all Refentše's mother's doing.

Cold facts stood unflinchingly before their eyes. Should they now kill Sammy as well? They had killed the innocent – twice. And, as Sammy himself had pointed out just the other day, if you could kill the innocent, then you had no business not to kill the guilty.

In the end, Sammy was spared the ordeal of death by stoning and fire. None of the Comrades was keen to kill a madman. Such a thing was, in fact, unheard of. There was a belief that any bad treatment of a mad person could lead to the abuser giving birth to an equally insane child. Even those who did not entirely share that belief were not prepared to risk the wrath of the Ancestors, or, simply, to stoop that low. Although one Comrade suggested that Sammy's madness was all pretence, nobody was carried away by that Comrade's insight.

The highlight of the whole meeting for Terror, though, was the revelation that precisely what he had warned Refentše about – and which the fellow in his self-righteous arrogance had dismissed – had, in fact, happened. And then, to crown it all, the fool had to go and commit suicide, as if there were no other women in the city!

On his way back to Johannesburg that Sunday afternoon after the meeting, Terror thought deeply about what he would say to Lerato. He smiled to himself. It was a quite unexpected and grand development, this madness of Sammy's. Terror had always known that at some stage in life, he would have his revenge. He intended to call Lerato the following morning, just in time to catch her before she left to attend her university classes. He experienced a certain grim pleasure in the thought that she would be forced to spend the rest of the morning, and more, thinking about him – he who was regarded as a dog, unworthy of any attention.

The following day duly arrived. The sun rose in the east, as it had done since time immemorial. It was cloudless and warm; Terror would not have to suffer any cold in order to realise his dreams. It was simply one of those rare mornings that even Terror, who did not usually care much about the weather, could receive with white hands.

He went to the telephone booth just across the street from his flat. Or, rather, from the flat he stayed in at unpredictable intervals, which he liked to call his. It, in fact, belonged to one of his Hillbrow sex objects.

All along the way, he thought about Refentše. There was something mentally wrong with this fellow villager who thought that life was about love and books only. The other problem with him had been that he could not take advice. Stirred by these thoughts came a memory, the memory of what Refentše had said to him the other day. The details rose in his memory like troubled sea waves in an ugly storm.

'Terror,' Refentše had said, 'Terror, I hope you are going to leave Sammy and Lerato alone. Who needs advice on love and friendship? Especially from you, who is known to be so untrustworthy with any woman? Please, do not take me for a fool. I know that you have tried to get sexual favours from Lerato. She told me. Now, you want to persuade me that Sammy is like you. No, Terror, I will not be advised by amoral people, who have no problem with going about raping prostitutes in Hillbrow. I believe I am seeing you for the last time in this flat.'

Terror was enraged. He had not expected Refentše to know, at least not so soon, about his latest scandal. He could have done anything to Refentše on the spot. Only, Refentše, for all his gentleness and kindness, did not swallow mud forced into his mouth by anyone. So Terror had to hesitate.

'You will remember me when the time comes,' was all he could say, as he banged the door closed behind him.

His thoughts were bitter as he left. So his most recent scandals were now known to everyone from Tiragalong who was in Johannesburg! Refentše, with his characteristically frank talk, would tell Sammy and Lerato about his banishment from the flat. Terror pictured Refentše embroidering the ugly story of his banishment with this latest piece of gossip. Terror had suffered various degrees of humiliation at home. But he shuddered when he thought about the intensity of what he would have to endure when he went home the next time. It brought to mind that other humiliation that he had endured at Refentše's instigation that day at school. And his contempt for Refentše was cemented.

But now his time had come. With Refentše dead and Sammy mad, he could subdue Lerato. He would play between her thighs as he had always wanted to do. All he would have to do was to let her know that her and Sammy's secret was now common knowledge in Tiragalong. It might not be the case in Hillbrow, or Alexandra, where her home was. But he would threaten to make it so if she did not provide for him what she had reserved for Refentše and Sammy for too long. The popular phrase doing the rounds in the country invaded his thoughts with hard strokes of cynicism: 'Redistribution of resources . . . '

But Terror did not have a full understanding of Lerato's contempt for him. When he had threatened to make it known to Lerato's mother what the real cause of Refentše's suicide was, Lerato's response had been to sigh deeply. Terror, from his telephone booth, had heard the sigh with a satisfied smile. For the first time things were taking shape in the way that he wanted.

For her part, Lerato worked out that, even in her most desperate state, she would never stoop to satisfy Terror's brutal desire. Or subject herself to his cruel madness. She thought deeply about the possibility of revealing to her mother her betrayal of Refentše. She knew that her mother would take the news badly, as she had liked her future son-in-law very much. It would be almost impossible for her to convince her mother that she was not really a murderess, and that she still loved Refentše deeply. There was no way that mother and daughter could live happily, or even tolerably, together after such a revelation.

Refentše's suicide had always lain heavily in her heart, even without the assistance of the further considerations that Terror's threat brought to bear on her brain. Soon, the campus would be buzzing with the story of the young woman whose voracious sexual appetite had led her into the streets of Hillbrow, in search of wandering penises that were prepared to come and caress her thighs. She imagined herself ground to the level of prostitute. There was no way she could look anyone in the eye now, and say: 'I am Lerato.'

Lerato sighed again. The sigh brought no relief, however, as she continued to live out her humiliation and suffering in her mind. All this, she thought, while Sammy basked in the sanctuary of his insanity.

Terror was to spit infinite blobs of bitter resentment onto the pavements of Hillbrow on learning, early the following day, that Lerato had followed in her lover's tracks.

Revived Memories

It was clear to the people of Tiragalong that Leruo was heading towards his death with dazzling speed. Elders clicked their tongues with concern. When they ventured audible words, it was a question, repeated often and never accompanied by any articulate answer, that formed the loudest part of their utterances.

'What's happening to children these days?' they asked, imploring the Ancestors to pardon the village if it was being punished for the wrongs it was not conscious of having committed.

The elders had every reason to be worried about their children. For how could any villager hope to benefit by marrying a Johannesburger? A long time ago, one villager had dared to marry a Jo'burg woman against the advice of his parents and all the other villagers. Or, rather, of those villagers who unashamedly made it their business to poke their noses into other people's affairs in the name of fellow feeling, only to turn the fellow feeling into a meaty source of gossip as soon as the object of their compassion had rounded the corner. Such villagers were numerous.

Now, this headstrong man of days past could not live with his wife happily. When the time was ripe enough, the villagers turned around and said to him: 'But we told you!'

The couple separated, mainly because the woman could not be persuaded to conform to the expectations of the village when it came to the position she held in her own family. Unlike most village women, she expected, among other things, that her husband should wash dishes for her while she cleaned the house. The man did not really have any serious reservations about doing women's chores. What bothered him was that the villagers began to spread the rumour that he must have swallowed an overdose of love potion. Even the most loving and tender of men in the village did not do such things, except, perhaps, when they were bewitched. The rumours went further: it was said that the remarkable success of the woman's love potion only showed that witchcraft was practised in the city as well, and that there was no civilisation anywhere.

These accusations of witchcraft were worrying to the couple. For if they continued, they would lead to the killing of the wife in the name of cleansing the village. The man refused to move with his wife to the city, to live there for the rest of their lives. He could not bring himself to prove to his fellow villagers that he had, indeed, swallowed hard doses of love potion, and have some of the villagers who worked in the city visit him regularly, with the express purpose of seeing for themselves how he handled witchcraft in the city. The wife, for her part, refused to be more lenient in her expectations of their responsibility towards each other. Sandwiched between the expectations of his beloved wife and the demands of the society he loved and respected, the man could not live happily at all. When he and his Johannesburger finally broke apart, with the wife choosing to live unthreatened in her home township of Alexandra, the popular opinion that Jo'burg women were no women at all was vindicated. As if that were not enough, the man lost his property in the subsequent divorce case.

It was under such conditions of first-hand knowledge of Jo'burg women that some of the villagers became concerned about Refentše's love relationship with a Jo'burg woman. Refentše's carelessness and rejection of the villagers' advice was said to result from reading too much. Because he was the most educated person in Tiragalong, so the story went, he thought that he was immune to the little sufferings and frustrations that any other villager could experience. Refentše and his lover fell out with each other when he discovered that she had had an affair with his best friend and fellow villager, Sammy. It was out of his disillusionment with friendship and love that Refentše committed suicide in Hillbrow, where he rented a flat.

Bits and pieces of intelligence as to the cause of the suicide finally found their way onto the N1 to Pietersburg, where Tiragalong was situated. The village refused to gather the pieces together and order them into a coherent story. Ten years after Refentše's death, Tiragalong would still insist that his suicide showed how bad the Jo'burg women were. Refentše's friend, Sammy, was known for his unquestionable integrity.

His betrayal of his friend could only have resulted from the seductive skills of the woman.

Now, Leruo appeared to think that it was his turn to follow in these worrying tracks. He began by doing what Tiragalong was convinced that, even in his worst moments of stubbornness, Refentše would not have done. The village looked on with consternation as Leruo chose a house in one of the wealthiest suburbs in the city. This was after the company he worked for had decided that it was time it offered him tenure and the generous housing subsidy that went with it.

Leruo had given careful thought to his choice. He had thought about the waste, money-wise, of owning a house in Tiragalong while he worked in the city. It was probable that he would visit the village only during holidays or over long weekends, now. There was no way he was going to live in his house in Tiragalong. And he saw no point in owning a house there, and renting a dwelling in the city. Besides, the value of the house in Tiragalong could not, even by the wildest stretch of imagination – and Leruo's imagination could be quite wild – compare favourably with a house in the northern suburbs of Jo'burg. In short, he thought that to choose to own a house in Tiragalong, in his circumstances, amounted to a glorification of impoverishment.

He saw no purpose whatsoever in living poorly when conditions were conducive to affluence. He could think of only two kinds of people who could afford to glorify poverty. One category comprised defeated people, who had to console themselves with the thought that their lot did not result from lack of trying to be otherwise. This group went to bed every night with a self-congratulatory pat on the shoulder because, as it claimed, at least it did not exploit other people for the sake of gaining wealth. The second group consisted of those born into wealth, who did not know what poverty was about. This latter group, despite its glorification of poverty, had no intention whatever of experimenting with the condition of poverty, or impoverishing itself for the sake of sharing in the so-called glory of it. This was a group very similar to a band of people who watched, fascinated, the various tricks displayed by a monkey, but without actually wishing that they could, by some chance, be the monkey themselves. Leruo did not see himself as belonging to either of these groups. It was considerations of this nature that made him feel that even though blood ties can be very thick, still he would not choose suffering for the sake of them.

But Tiragalong saw his choice from a different angle. The villagers lost bucketfuls of saliva as they spat with disgust at the notion of this haughty young man whose contempt for them was so strong that he could not even live among them.

Leruo was in Standard Six when Refentše died. He had felt the death severely. For Refentše was more than a cousin to him, he was also a friend. He used to spend much time with Leruo, during his university holidays, teaching Leruo many things. It was Refentše who impressed on Leruo's mind that when he matriculated he should go on to study at university.

It was largely because of their friendship, rather than their cousinship, that Leruo spent most of his school holidays in Tiragalong, at Refentše's home. Leruo's home was actually in the neighbouring village of Nnoko. But he spent sufficient time in Tiragalong for the people there tacitly to regard him as one of themselves and to convince themselves that when he became an adult he was going to live in Tiragalong. It was assumptions of this nature that led Tiragalong to take particular interest in him when he matriculated with flying colours. He had a reputation for being a good child, then.

What made Leruo want to study at the university in the South was that his cousin had studied there, and also taught there for just above two months before his suicide. He did not know how Refentše had discovered this university, as the few village youths who were eligible to enter a university after matric usually went to the University of the North, located only a stone's throw from their village, while most read for their teachers' diplomas in the colleges around Pietersburg. As he went through his secondary schooling, Leruo grew interested to know a bit more about Refentše's university. It was his class teacher who wrote to the university for information on the courses on offer. And it was with satisfaction that Leruo learnt that the university offered the kind of subjects he was interested in studying.

But it was more out of sentimental attachment to his late cousin, and because he dared to be different from the other village youths, that Leruo resolved to go and study there. His decision had very little to do with respect for that particular university. For Leruo did not know enough about universities, then, to be able to compare them.

Once at the university, Leruo did as well as anyone who knew him could expect. He was awarded scholarships from his first year of study right through to his final year. Because he did so extremely well, and because sponsors often favoured students of commerce and industry, the scholarships he applied for simply came tumbling into his student account. When, after four years of intensive study, he began to work as an accountant, he was already a wealthy young man. At least by the village standards, if not by any other.

During his first year of employment with the company, he lived comfortably in a rented flat in Parktown, while he waited patiently for the following year, when his company would make house and car subsidies available to him.

It was in the year that the company's generosity flowed over him that he fell in love with the woman who subsequently came to be his much-despised wife. Despised, that is, not by him, but by the people of Tiragalong, most of whom had not even met her yet, nor had any desire to meet her. Except, should the chance present itself, to spit all the disgust in which they held her into her face.

Beth was lecturing at a college of education, then. Having been Leruo's classmate throughout their university days, she had decided to enrol for her Masters degree in the year that Leruo began to work. They had remained close friends throughout that time, and they saw each other often. Their friendship was further cemented when they opened up towards each other a little more than usual one day. It was Beth who began it, by asking the question that she had kept to herself for some time. She had wanted to share this with Leruo for a long while. But it was a somewhat sensitive subject, as it involved her sister's death. It was the pressing desire to communicate it and to see how her trusted friend – whose trust she had not tested before – would behave after her revelations, that finally led to her daring.

'I hope you are not too patriotic, Leruo?'

'Well, try me.'

'I mean, I hope you will not be hurt by what I have to say. You don't mind people saying bad things about your fellow villagers when they have good reason to talk that way about them?'

Leruo raised the tips of his ears at this. Beth had never said or done anything to hurt him before. Nor had it ever occurred to him that she was capable of it. Also, this apologetic manner towards him was something new. He had every reason to listen with interest. Still, he did not want to appear to be too curious. So he said something to the effect that you only knew whether something was hurtful once it had hurt you already.

Beth had smiled in her usual dismissal of his gentle cynicism.

'You see, until last year I did not know that Tiragalong was my home too. Or, rather, it was my sister's home, even though she didn't know it. For reasons I don't quite understand my mother suddenly decided to drown me with the history of our family.'

Leruo wondered why Beth should have difficulty understanding her mother's decision to tell the family history. After all, was that not what all good parents were supposed to tell their children? If there was anything incomprehensible, he thought, it would be that the history had to wait until last year to be revealed.

In the middle of wondering about this, Leruo still could not help listening with unabashed attention.

Beth's story was long. It was not entertaining, but it added chunks of knowledge to what Leruo already knew about her.

She told Leruo that her elder sister, Lerato, was once in love with a young man from Tiragalong. His name was Refentše. Now, it appeared that Refentše had serious personal problems. So serious were they, in fact, that he could not communicate them to anyone. Lerato included. When his situation failed to improve, he found that the only solution to the headaches the problems caused him would be for him to jump from the balcony of his flat, and crush himself against the street.

Since Lerato never got to know what the problem was, she naturally felt very betrayed. She spent a lot of time, just after the suicide, brooding over what could have caused her lover to betray her in this way. She could not exclude the possibility that she might have contributed towards the suicide, somehow.

One day Beth's mother returned from work late in the evening, so the story continued, only to find that Lerato had swallowed numerous poisonous tablets. Beth had gone to Durban to visit a relative at the time. She had to return in a hurry when she received a telephone message informing her about her sister's departure to the underworld.

The mother could only attribute Lerato's suicide to her unbearable grief at her lover's senseless death. For Lerato was such a good person that the mother could not fathom any other likely explanation for her self-destruction.

Beth closed her narrative by saying that the mother's horrible discovery that evening had reminded her of the difficulties she had encountered in bringing her two daughters up alone. It also intensified the resentment she felt at the premature death of Lerato's father, who was stabbed to death in Alexandra for reasons nobody had yet established. The result was that the mother had nobody, now, who was intimate enough to share with, in the real sense of sharing, the pain of Lerato's departure. It seemed to her, then, that she was destined to witness major misfortunes for the rest of her life.

'It seems that Lerato's father came from Tiragalong,' Beth told Leruo. As if in an afterthought she added that, at the time of her father's death, Lerato was still curled snugly in her mother's womb.

Leruo thought, now, that he could understand why Beth's mother had not been able to tell her daughter their family story until recently. It was a painful story, of the kind that one was not necessarily sure should be told to children. The kind that, even when one decided to tell it, one might not know how to tell.

But since the story had come out, finally, and since Beth had trusted him enough to be able to confide in him, Leruo tried to complete the picture by telling Beth what he knew. He was grateful to be able to associate Lerato with someone that he knew. Not entirely happy, though, because Beth was such a dear and decent soul to him, in contrast to what Lerato had been to his cousin. But at least Lerato was no longer a mysterious existence that circulated only in the mouths of the villagers. She began, even if in her grave, to have a solid presence in his mind. Now, in her turn, Beth might be interested to have something added to her family story, Leruo thought.

Beth's surprise was enormous when she learnt that Refentše was, in fact, Leruo's cousin. Leruo seldom talked about him, as he explained, because he was always trying hard to suppress the ever-depressing memory of his cousin's suicide.

Leruo went on to say that, although he was not in any position to explain Lerato's decision to follow her lover into the grave, to his knowledge Lerato and Refentše had broken up on the day that Refentše died. It was common knowledge in the village that, at the time, Lerato was in love with Refentše's friend. How long this secret affair had been going on before Refentše found out, Leruo could not say.

Leruo hesitated a little before he drew the curtain back further on his side of the story.

'And . . . well . . . it might be that it was this friend who left Lerato in the cold.'

This was a picture that was painfully different from the one that Beth and her mother had carried. The revision of the knowledge that Beth had of her sister left her heart bleeding. Her eyes gradually filled with tears, which did not appear too intent on rolling down her cheeks. She could not be sure whether it was sympathy for her sister, or condemnation of Lerato's behaviour that caused her heart to be filled with such an ache.

Leruo read her acute distress from her face. At the sight of her emotion, his long-suppressed love for her weighed heavily upon him. It was as if his heart carried a bagful of stones. He stood up slowly from his chair, stretched himself and pretended to yawn, all the while striving to find something good to say to her. Walking up to her, he stood in front of her with a pained smile, while words continued to elude him. Beth smiled back. Quickly, unexpectedly, she stood up and while Leruo was still trying to find the elusive right words to say to her, she planted a kiss on his lips. Impulsively, Leruo locked his hands around her body, all the while simultaneously aware of his nagging feeling of uncertainty.

He was not sure whether he had behaved well by causing cracks in the shell of Beth's idealised picture of her sister. He was full of regret that he had had to crush her spirits, just when she had begun to open up to him in a way that she had not done before.

For her part, Beth felt that she had insight for the first time into who Leruo was. And, for this knowledge and his openness, she liked him more than ever.

The expressive silence that culminated in their mutual embrace during that delicate moment was to become a source of juicy chats between the lovers in later days of reminiscence.

Tiragalong was not there to witness the two hearts melting and flowing into each other. The first inklings of gossip about this newly found relationship derived from the enthusiastic tongues of the village migrants who worked in the city. Right from the start the issue was simple in the eyes of the villagers. Like most of the youths who went to study in the big city, with the possible exception of only one or two, this child of the soil had fallen, inevitably, into the intricate snares laid down for him by the Jo'burg vultures.

'They will all pretend to love him. He's wealthy, after all,' Tiragalong whispered.

It took a very short time before the whispers became audible, and grew ever noisier, as the village learnt more about Beth.

The first lesson was that she was a lecturer.

'Ha!' Tiragalong could not hold back the exclamation.

For, the combination of education and womanhood in a Johannesburger could only point to imminent disaster. It was more than enough that Beth, like all Johannesburgers, would not understand and appreciate their culture. Added to this was the fact that there could be no hope of ever teaching her anything. Educated women had minds that were too full of books to accommodate anything else. Even educated village women were known to make extremely impoverished wives, as there were things they simply refused to do. What could the village make, for example, of a twenty-five-year-old woman who was so lazy that she had to employ another villager of her mother's age to do housework for her? When all the time she herself was right there in her house, sitting at a table and reading!

It took some time before the village learnt that Beth was Lerato's sister. Tiragalong recalled Refentše's suicide and the gloom that had hung over the village for a long time afterwards. And when Leruo chose a house in a Jo'burg suburb, people could not but be reminded that even city dwellers practised witchcraft. There were those villagers who recalled that Leruo chose the house that was his before he and Beth became the bones of each other's hearts. But even these individuals were brought to doubt their own judgement. Cynicism overrode memory, and suggestions that their love must have had a longer history in secret, took root. So it was that Leruo's choice of location was attributed to nothing other than his new love. Especially to her evil art. It was crystal clear to all that Leruo had swallowed an overdose of I-am-the-only-one, the love potion that made men believe that the only good words and decisions were the ones said and taken by their lovers. This was confirmed by the fact that under normal circumstances, men do not allow themselves to be pulled by the noses, especially by a woman, where such grave choices are concerned.

Beth and Leruo's subsequent marriage could only aggravate the village's already sufficiently brooding memory.

Interlude: Memories Of Brooding

memories of brooding bruise
the ailing heart
the bruised heart hiding
in the blooming flower in the jungle
of our discontent
as the glaring ember
fries our hearts from blue heavens
hot passions of love bloom like flowers
in spring only to melt evaporate
then condense into brooding clouds
we jostle our way through showers of rain that soak
the land with baffled hopes
hopes of shrill voices & sharp gazes once certain
of the certainty of our diminishing love
baffled
we too look on at the deep fountains of sweet love
quivering in the violent flow
of voices & gazes disrupting the rhythmic melody
of singing hearts & we remember
we remember those memories of joy that once floated
in the calm air almost oblivious to the world
around it

Love, Songs & Blues

Sereto Sa Phaswane Mogano*

Ke Kupša Mahlakwane a Nkhona
Ke Phaswane a Mmalesiba mogale moihlabanedi
A re Kupša o thulame
O ye o botše ba ga-Masemola Magadimane
Ba tšwe ba tšhabe
Nna Kupša phodisa sa Morišane ga-Mphahlele
Ke re go tsena ka kgoro tša Mauba
Ba šwahle magora ba tšhabe
Ke re bašang gagešo molato ge o le kgorong
Ga re bitše basadi
Mohla re bitša basadi
Re re šilang matsoku le ba alošeng
Ke Kupša morwa Manabile a Sefata Matlala
A koto la ka ga le na bosese
Ke swana yeo e tšwago Modue ga-Rauwane
Ya tabola Konyama ya bethela Mokgoroma ka thoko
Ke ya ga-Lepogo la Moruakgomo a Lebotša
A re kgomo ke thopa tše dikhwebedu
Tše tšhweu ke tšhaba mebala
Ke Lepogo ke Ilane ke Ilane a Mahlako
Ke phefo sefopha madimo
Ya tabola Moletši Moletši ya šala e le marope
Manala wee . . . Manala a boputla bja kgomo

* 'Praise Poem of Phaswane Mogano'. This poem was originally composed in Sepedi by Phaswane. The English version, with translation provided by Nape 'a Motana, appears on the following page.

Praise Poem Of Phaswane Mogano[1]

I am Kupša Mahlakwane of Nkhona[2]
I, Phaswane of Mmalesiba, brave warrior standing his ground
with own spears
Say: Kupša, go down
Go and tell the Masemola Magadimane clan
To come out and flee
Kupša, powerful healer of Morišane at ga-Mphahlele village
When I enter the gates of Mauba's[3] court
They penetrate the hedge and flee
I declare: Hey you weak-kneed fledglings
At my homestead when there is a case at the men's court
We don't invite women
When we call women we say
Grind the ochre and bring back the initiates[4]
I, Kupša son of Manabile of Sefata Matlala
Who insists my foot is not narrowly shaped[5]
I'm the dark hero who hails from Modue of Rauwane
Who runs and leaps over Konyama, pushing Mokgoroma
onto the wayside
On my way to Lepogo village belonging to Maruakgomo of Lebotša
He states: As for cattle, I only capture the red ones[6]
I am afraid of the colours of the white ones
I am Lepogo, I am Ilane, I am Ilane of Mahlako[7]
I am a wind, a breaker of storms
When it descends on Moletši, Moletši becomes ruins
Hello, Manala . . . Manala of the cattle-crossing spot[8]

Notes

1. This poem and the following one, 'St Bede's High', have been written according to izibongo or praise-poem conventions, which weave in heroic personal achievements with references to family lineage and shared communal experiences. Explanations have been suggested for some of the lines, but the complexity and density of the symbolism makes it difficult to attempt any too exact meaning. Many of the references are very personal and have a metaphoric significance that only the poet would be able to unravel.
2. Nkhona is the father of Mahlakwane, who is the father of Kupša.
3. Mauba is a praise name for people who reside in the Sekhukhune area.
4. Refers to the male initiates attending initiation school in the mountains.
5. In other words, 'I do not have the foot of a weakling; I am a powerful man'.
6. Red cattle are harder to identify from a distance, since they blend in with the soil and thus are less likely to be spotted by the owner. But the reference could also be to the red ochre that signifies the successful completion of initiation.
7. Lepogo is 'Leopard', and Ilane is possibly one of the poet's heroic names, 'The One Who Roars'.
8. Refers to the captured cattle, crossing over into the village of heroes. Manala is a name given to an initiation school, the implication being the triumphant return of the initiates from the hard 'battle' of koma or initiation.

St Bede's High*

tswala yona e bile gona
ngwan'a mokgalabje wa batho
gobane o se pudi yela ya go re mokaka o kae
re ile go tšwa tharing ya mokgekolo
ra ikela aretse kgolekgole
moo merafo ya gauta e re tomoletšego maahlo
go tswala o tswetše hle bede yo mokgethwa
fela o tswaletše eng ge e se gauteng
gobane mono gae komelelo ruriruri
e iphile maatla

le ge go le bjalo re a amogela
gobane go se amogele ke ga eng
gobane le wena kgetho o e hlokile
le ge go le bjalo re a amogela
re re ke nnete gore monakana o re tšheletše
ruriruri bede motho wa kgoobe
ge o ikadile bjalo maotong a magagamatala
ke go lebelela ke kgapha dikeledi
ke emetše gore ge le tshela kgomo mokokotlo
lepapate ke tope ke hlabe mokgoši
gobane ke tshwanelo gore afrika borwa e fiwe
e amogele leo le rego ke yola mothomotho
yena ngwan'a ntepa ya tshadi
le 'šete la poo
dipuku re lle ra nwa hle mothopo wa rena

* This poem was originally composed in Sepedi by Phaswane. The English version, with translation provided by Nape 'a Motana, appears on the following page.

St Bede's High

As for birth, it has happened,
child of the old man,
for you are not goat without udder.[1]
we emerged from the thari[2] of old woman
and went to unknown far-far places,
where gold-digging throngs are gazing at us with unfriendly looks.
giving birth, you have given birth o holy bede
but you gave birth for what if not for gauteng[3]
for here at home drought has indeed become rampant.

nevertheless we accept
because you did not have a choice
nevertheless we still accept
saying, it is true you have given to us,
indeed, bede the pregnant one sprawling
to the legs of green meadows,
when I gaze at you I shed tears of joy.
i am waiting for the sun to scorch a cow's spine
then I shall blow the horn and ululate
for it is fitting that south africa should be given
and receive wise words.
a person-to-the-core, product of an ntepa-wearing[4] woman
and the bull's testicle,[5] has a weight of worth.
books we ate and drank, o our ever-flowing fountain

1. You are not a goat whose reason for not giving birth is a tiny udder.
2. A carry-cot, usually made from a goat's hide.
3. Refers to the province of Gauteng, which is also the Sotho name for Johannesburg, 'Place of Gold'.
4. Ntepa is a short skirt made of tanned animal hide that used to be worn by Bapedi women and girls.
5. He is human in the fullest sense of the word, blood child of a 'real' woman and man.

Moyana Wa Matsikinyane*

ke lebelela
maru a go phatlalala ge a kgobokanela
legala leo le fisago
leo le kgabaganyago magodimong a botalalerata
letsopa leo le palegilego la tiragalong
le a tsitsila le lla ka el nino el nino
maru a maso a betsa ntakana ya go hloka pelohlomogi
go maahlo a go kgopela mogau
mola meetsefula a betsa makwate a mobu
ka nokeng yeo e hlatsago
mola mafula a mahlomola
a kgameletsa moyana wa matsikinyane
wa naga yeo e ikadilego
gomme leruo leo le tsietswago
ke marapotshokgo a magagaboona
ge a bonala diiponeng tsa go pshatlega
fasefase mawatleng a letsopa
moo meetse nkabego a le gona
le re mmu le re mmee . . .
le goeleletsa khutso ye tala
gore e tle gona bjalo . . .

June 1998
Berea, Johannesburg

* Phaswane's Sepedi adaptation of 'The Open Air'. The English original can be found in the *Brooding Clouds* short story section on p. 2.

Imagined Walk

let's take this walk
through the lush greenness
of tiragalong's mealie fields
before the drought
the el nino catches
up with us
let's take this green walk
bone of my heart
before the guts of my heart
spill over into the sweet gleam
of hillbrow's neon lights
where i glimpsed
my other love yesternight

May 1998
Berea, Johannesburg

Marapo A Pelo*

a re sepele
re kgabaganye botala bja go loya
bja masemo a tiragalong a mafela
pele komelelo el nino
e re fihlela
a re sepele la mafelelo
lerapo la pelo ya ka
pele mateng a pelo ya ka
a kgothogela ka seeding se sebosana
sa mabone a hillbrow
moo ke fahlogetsego lerapo le lengwe
la pelo ya ka
bosegong bja maabane

June 1998
Berea, Johannesburg

* Phaswane's Sepedi adaptation of 'Imagined Walk'.

Little Bee Buzzing

i watch that bee
buzz buzzing over the geraniums
hovering above them
& constantly
digging its tube into the flower
& its little head
emerging
with excited satisfaction
buzz . . . resumes the droning song
of my unrequited love
constantly digging furrows
in my aching heart
& feeding on the sweat
of my brooding brain
trying to rest
within the encasing skull

May 1998
Berea, Johannesburg

Wa Papa*

ke wena motho wo
wa papa
ke neng ke hlahlatha le menagano
ke hlahlathisa maoto
ke tseba gabotsebotse
bohloko bja lerato
ge le timeletse
fela o hweditswe
wa mma
o hweditswe
o . . . o . . .
o hweditswe o tsikinyana
le meago ya malekeleke
ya hillbrow

May 1998
Berea, Johannesburg

* Phaswane's Sepedi adaptation of 'My Pa Se Kind'. The English original can be found on p. 31.

Here We Meet Child Of Home

we bump into each other
at the head of kotze street
a shock of recognition wells in my heart
like muddled seas
under grim guidance of raging storms
displaying their strength
& power against each other
so you're here my neighbour's child
tiragalong has reported you lost
in the last decade
reported you lost & determined rumours
said you died . . .
said you crushed under the heavy bullets
of flying squads rescuing cash security
from an ugly heist you hoisted
near oom kruger's statue
we sang *we're just passers-by*
on this earth of milk & honey
& blood washing down the dirt
in the streets of pretoria
& hillbrow & crimson memories
swimming through telephone lines
& N1 to find their nest in tiragalong
we sang woeful tales & said
how good you were in your school days
just before wild dreams of youth
bombarded you with visions
of gleams of sanctuary & bliss in the city
that gapes with gold mines
some said it could only have been witchcraft
driving your grey matter
& we said that too was true

for we knew your step-parent sent the hide whip
negotiating its way over your bare shoulders
without a cause & your heartrending screams
brought no remorse to the heart
of failed parenthood finding heavenly sanctuary
in chilling screams of innocent youth
you're found my pa se kind
but ma is dead now
spared this sight of glue splattered across your face
& glassy eyes failing to recognise
my shocked presence & lice milling into
& out your rags & the fearsome forest
of hair on your head
pa died too . . .
died chasing underwaist bliss in quartz street
his guts ripped open by his cousin
who thought he owned hillbrow
until hillbrow high life
snarled at him tore his skull
into messy fragments of bones
painted red & grey
& you too were spared the painful sight
of pa's bleached bones brooding over hillbrow
i wonder at your uncaring silence as i greet you
child of the soil of tiragalong
then . . . then with a searing pain
i realise whatever i do
& say will never pull you out
of that world of glue that spins in your brains
so i move on trying to see the world
through the eyes of a child who sees
it through the eyes of glue

July 1998
Berea, Johannesburg

In The Depths Of Sleep

i roll over
the left side relieving the right
listening to exhaustion
that spreads itself
all over
negotiating the curves
of my bodyscape
pounding into the depths of flesh
& sucking in the marrow of the brain
i see you coming nearer
with the smile
of a successful witch
your scaly body
wrapped around the waist
of a horned monster
i shudder
at the thought
of your kissing me in the light
of my dreams
of your cock . . . concubine
spitting poisonous juices
gathered from the thighs of whoredom
into the hole
of my womanhood
but i let love
roll away soothing words
from the waggling tongue
disguise the deep pain
of broken love
steadying itself against storms

of mockery
of love seeking satisfaction
in quartz
& returning only with handfuls
of deepening nightmares
your face
once so smooth & tender
is now furrowed
by deep thoughts of shattered family
of the little one
yelling daddy to your homeboy
that plays his games
between my thighs
he too haunts
the depths of my sleep jeers
at the little one
he hugs & with warmth
kisses the bone
of his heart
before my eyes
mama i thought he was daddy
he is child
but she is not mummy
perhaps she is child
child
oh child
maybe when you're grown up
& you see shades of life
& love
you'll love us still
love us for teaching you motherhood
& fatherhood
& other hoods

in this garden of blooming sensuality
& baffled rationality
in which we die chasing
happiness
& even after we're departed
the flowers of love
flourish
under the care of homeboys
& homegirls
perhaps you'll love us still
child
if you listened
but oh baby
you scream me into wakefulness
& memories of our love
jolt me back
into the gloom of preceding moments
& the mellow days
when we knew
love was love

April 1998
Berea, Johannesburg

Mateng-Teng A Boroko*

ke a retologa
lehlakore la ntsogohlo le khutsisa la go ja
ke theeleditse molapo
ge o ikala gohlegohle
o potologa le dikhutla
tsa mmejana wa ka
o tsenelela mateng a digoba tsa mmele
gomme a inwela mmoko wa mabjoko
ke go bona o batamela
ka monywanywo bjalo ka moloi
woo a tswelago go latswa katlego
mmele wa gago wa magapi
o ithareditse nokeng
ya sebata sa dinaka
ke kwa ke tsiroga ge ke nagana
gore o tlo nkatla mo leseding
la ditoro tsa ka
ke nagana gore makadi a gago . . . mokaolana wa gago
o tshwela meetsana a dienywa a mpholo
mosimeng
wa bosadi bja ka
fela ke dumelela lerato
le lokolla mantsu a mamapo
go tswa lelemeng la leemaema
ke siretsa bohloko bja go tsetsemetsa
bja lerato ge le thubegile

* Phaswane's Sepedi adaptation of 'In The Depths Of Sleep'.

le itiseletsa kgahlanong le madimo
a tlaiso
bja lerato le tsomana le kgotsofalo
ka quartz
gomme le bowa le tlhobaelo
ya go tlala seatla
sefahlego sa gago
sa boreletsana se se nanana
bjalo se tswele mekero
se epilwe ke menagano ya lapa ge le thubega
ke go gopola ka ngwana
a goeletsa papa go mogageno
woo a bapalago dipapadi tsa gagwe
kgahlo ga dirope tsa ka
le yena mogageno o hlobaetsa
boteng bja boroko bja ka
o hlobaetsa ngwana
o gokara a bile a atla
lerapo la pelo ya gagwe ka borutho
pele ga maahlo a ka
mma ke be ke re anthe ke papa
ke yena ngwan'aka
fela wola ga se mma
mohlomongwe ke yena ngwan'aka
ngwan'aka
hle ngwan'aka
mohlomongwe ge o gotse
o bone meriti ya bophelo
le lerato
o tla no tswela pele ka go re rata
wa re ratela go go ruta bo-mme
le bo-papa
le bo-aretse

mo serapaneng sa maikutlo a go thunya
le menagano ya kgakanego
serapaneng seo go sona re hwago re kitimisa
lethabo
gomme le ge re sepetse
matsoba a lerato a sala
a thunya
tlhokomeng ya bowarra
le bokgaetsedi
mohlomongwe o tla no tswela pele wa re rata
ngwan'aka
ge o ka theeletsa
fela ngwan'aka
kgoeletso ya gago e mpusa lefaseng
la ba go hlobaela mpeng ya leswiswi
gomme megopolo ya lerato la rena
e nkgogela leswiswing la mohlamonene
le matsatsing a dinose
ge re be re sa tseba
lerato e le lerato

June 1998
Berea, Johannesburg

X-Mas Love Songs

the sun
dancing in the east
casts light on scorpions
of the mind
as migrant arrives
& a neighbour's jacket tail
vanishes out the window
brooding clouds the heart
& the floating song evaporates
skulls crack & break
under mighty blows
of filed axes
it is the migrant denying woeful tales
of visits to chelsea
& quirinalle whorehouses
the bone of the heart collapses
while screaming no aids
no aids . . .
the migrant spread like a pumpkin plant
bred like a rabbit
quartz street teems with offspring
now displaying wares
in whorehouses
migrant plunges butcher knives into the guts
of fellow villagers over drops of his blood
claiming a share
of underground bliss
news finally hitting N1
via pietersburg to the homestead
sweetie's hopes of a better tomorrow crush

in head-on collision
with the news
daydreaming melts & flows
into screaming nightmares
neighbour jumps out blankets
& over the fence while sweetie lies in hospital
the first coming that would knot
chains of love
stoking the hot stove between the thighs
manhood thrust forward yields
agonised moans
no despair no despair yet
honey . . .
until migrant lands
with thunderous wrath
& wakes up to his loose hold
on the homestead
turns over the pages of his life to find
the concrete pavements
of hillbrow
& the open air of the countryside
& no sanctuary
in either

December 1997
Brixton, Johannesburg

The Picture

i lift it up
bring it closer to my blurred vision
& kiss it fondly
waves jump up
& down in the sea
of my heart's depths
they bounce against the shores & fall back
torrents of passion ensnared
within the heart's kraal
bone of my heart
i dish out smiles
smile back at the smile
on your soft gentle lips
& the kindly heart that throws sweet smiles
toward the corners of hillbrow
& tiragalong
& opening my eyes in the gloom of night
i catch the grey matter wondering
in your unannounced turbulent absence
who is he whose nights are blessed
with quiet nightmareless sleep
& as hillbrow & tiragalong melt into each other
before my eyes in the dark
i embrace caress & kiss the solution
good night . . .

December 1997
Brixton, Johannesburg

The Love Beyond

daddy's gone
behind those mountains
but mother how does he go there
where the mountains
& the skies
meet
i try to look
for a crack
but the lush greenness
of the mountains
& the bright blueness
of the heavens
have shut the crevice down
but then daddy is gone
gone forever
to meet
his other love
beyond
the mountains

May 1998
Berea, Johannesburg

Mosong Wola*

tate o iketse mosol'a dithaba
mma a ka ya bjang fao
mola dithaba le leratadima di kopana
ke leka go nyaka lerwa ka maahlo
fela botalamorogo bja go nona bja dithaba
le botalalerata bja go phadima bja magodimo
a tswaletse lerwa
fela tate o ile . . . o iketse sa ruri
go kopana le lerapo le lengwe
la pelo ya gagwe
ka mosol'a wa dithaba

June 1998
Berea, Johannesburg

* Phaswane's Sepedi adaptation of 'The Love Beyond'.

Matsogo*

ke bala mo
leswiswing la go hlahlatha
peleng
ke be ke re re a reresa
ge le lomana ga bonolo
mo melaleng
ge re re le el nino
yeo e tlabilego balemi
ke ngwana go lerato la rena la go fihla marung
ga go gonontshe
gore lerato re be re le swinne
lerapo la pelo ya ka
fela bjalo ka limpopo
morago ga mafula a pula
ge a khutsisa
magodimo a maso
lerato le ile la fufula
noka e ile ya tshwela
mahlatsa a yona
ka maleng
a meboya ya go bolawa ke tlala
yeo e llelago lerato
ka seterateng sa quartz
lerato la pelo ya ka
o be o se nosi
mo go khurupolleng diatla

* Phaswane's Sepedi adaptation of 'When I Am Awake'. The English original can be found on p. 47.

le nna ke e sotse menywanywo
ke e sola bjalo ka legala
ge le fela le dira mesong ya lehlabula
ge le hlaba ka maahlo a botho
dithabeng tsa bohlabela
bjalo ke nna wo
ke wo ke bala mo leswiswing
ke e na le seamus deane . . .
deane a leka ka maatla
go bala lebalabalo la ka
mola monago wo o hlobaelago
le maikutlo a go kgabakgaba
a tshabela tebelelo
ya maahlo a go tsenelela
ke bala mo leswiswing
ke bala go se be gona ga gago
ke ipotsisa gore wena o balang
le ge ke tseba gore le waen
o swanetse go no ba o bala mo leswiswing
o ipotsisa gore re be re re re dira'ng
ge re sola lerato
tseo o ka rego
ke dijo

June 1998
Berea, Johannesburg

Visions Of Joy

child
wipe away those floods
of tears
digging furrows
in your cheeks
we're together now
daddy died chasing happiness
between the thighs
of whoredom
whoredom written in strokes
of everlasting greenness
he stood at the top of a hill
overlooking endless stretches
of greenery
so well grown
his eyes missed the brown earth
in between the tufts of grass
he searched with a keen eye
searched
& searched . . .
eyes floating over the greenery
further from where his feet stood firmly
i implored with soft eyes
for that tender attention
his heart was often so brimful of
but child
daddy had to send the searching eyes
beyond the nearby clod
of my presence
for the stretches beckoned
& his village

clothed me in new attire
said i was a witch
come to push
love potions
down his eager throat
& he said
yes
child once stones were edible
& trees could walk
& bones of the heart
radiated warm brilliance
once the heart & brain
were unclouded
by herbal dosage
of haunted anxiety
of loving losing hold
of itself
of faith disintegrating
in the gloom
of winter
knocking at the heart's door
feeling the chill
of misgiving brains
splattering themselves across the heart
child
wipe away the tears
daddy had to seek
happiness
beyond these moments
of witchery

April 1998
Berea, Johannesburg

Dipono Tsa Lethabo*

ngwan'aka
phumola mafula ao
a meokgo
a epago mekero
marameng
ke mo re go tee ngwan'aka
tatago o hwile a salane le lethabo morago
a kitimisa lethabo kgahlo ga dirope
sa bokobabane
bokababane bja go ngwalwa ka bokgabo
bja botalamorogo bja go hloka bofelo
o ile a ema sehloreng sa mmoto
woo o ukametsego
botala
bja go gola ka tshwanelo moo e lego gore
maahlo o gagwe a ile a tshela bosehla bja mobu
bja go patlama kgahlo ga mesehlo ya go siwa ke mabjang
o ile a nyaka ka leihlo le ntshontsho
o nyakile
a nyaka . . .
maahlo a gagwe a phophometse botaleng
thokwana go tloga moo maoto a gagwe
a bego a metse go tsenelela
ke mo kgopetse ka maahlo
ke kgopela gore a nkele tlhoko
yeo pelo ya gagwe e bego e fela e phophoma ka yona
fela ngwan'aka

* Phaswane's Sepedi adaptation of 'Visions of Joy'.

tatago o ile a no romela maahlo a go tsoma
kgojana le lekwate la kgauswi
la go ba gona ga ka
gobane mogola o be o ikadile o bile o goga maahlo
gomme motsana wabo
o nkapesitse ka se seswa seaparo
o re ke moloi
ke tlile go kitela
meratiso
kgolokgolong ya gagwe ya go ratela
yena a ba a re
ee . . .
peleng maswika a be a le boleta
gomme mehlare e sepela
mola marapo a pelo
a taga
ka seetsa se borutho
pelo le mabjoko
di be di sa pipes ke maru
a mokgatholo wa mereana
ya poifo ya go thuthumela
ya lerato ge le itimelela
ya tshepo ge e thubega
leswiswing
la marega
a go kokota lebating la pelo
e le ge e bolawa ke tonyo
ya mabjoko a go itlhoboga
ge a ikgasantsha mafahleng
ngwan'aka
phumola meokgo
tatago o be a swanetse a nyakane
le lethabo

ka mosola wa mehla ya nako yeo
ya boloi

June 1998
Berea, Johannesburg

Singing The Blues

i'm the blues in you
reminding you
of the heydays
of your youth
i'm a foetus that you threw
into & deserted in mother's womb
shot out the gaol
of placenta
& dived into hillbrow
high life
grown into a pimp
i now haunt the selfserving
smile
of your social work existence
taking care
of street kids

April 1998
Braamfontein, Johannesburg

In The Heat Of The Day

bang bang bang
screams of scuttling crowds
give birth to hysteria
the sonorous drone
of the priest's prayers
drown in the jarring snaps
of gunshots
amen is suspended midway
while the mind
impulsively checks with the shoes
can they carry the body away
from this place of death
in a moment of overflowing anger
a comrade screams
catch the bastard
& down goes the comrade
a hungry bullet having pierced through
& dashed to pieces
the heart of his heart
another angry comrade
totes his gun
the police waiting for reinforcements
watch from a safe distance
at this battle of guns
competing for our attention
as gangsters celebrate the death of their comrade
& comrades dream
of ending the reign of terror
& the police still wait
& watch

the frightened township crowds
scuttle in all corners
of the cemetery
praying in earnest
with their sore hearts
stuck in their throats
stifling further cries
& the sun gushing out rays of merciless heat
scorching moulds
of soil & whistling crickets
& baking away the green dreams
of hope of a better life
& so the funeral
comes to an abrupt end
with our hope
that he shall see a better life
on the other side of life

May 1998
Berea, Johannesburg

Time To Rest

it's an eyesore
at usindiso city shelter
i look at him leaning against the brown & cream wall
of the shelter
violent fits of coughing wreck the frail frame
& drown the eyes with water
tears trickle down the dark face
to meet the drooling spindle in the hairy forest
at the tip of the chin
aibo aibo he screams
for my other attention
attending its own little miseries
fumbling with the guts of my trousers
i throw up pocket linings
perturbed i try my hand at a smile
& agee ntate
a smile shoots out the brooding clouds
that hover around his face
thank you i hear him say
as i move on
the depths of my heart overflowing
with a searing longing
longing to return to the warmth of smiles
that defy those clouds of brooding
locked in a chilling embrace
with concrete towers of hillbrow
the wall stands there still
though without its complement
aibo i hear my heart scream
as intimations of graves

flood my blood stream
& as the heat in the streams
boils me into wakefulness
i swear that i know
i know it's a heartsore
that wall
without the smile . . .

January 1998
Berea, Johannesburg

Nako Ya Maikhutso*

go thonkga maahlo
kua usindiso city shelter
ke mo lebeletse ge a ithekgile
ka leboto le letsotho le bosweu
la boiphihlo bjoo
mogohlolo wo mosoro wa sentsokela
o kgohlakgohlisa mmejana wa go se be gona
mola o bile o kgamisa maahlo ka meetse
megokgo e elela go theoga le sefahlego se seso
go tla go kopana le ditete
tsa go iketla kua sethokgweng sa boya
ntlheng ya seledu
aibo aibo o a goeletsa
o nyaka kelatlhoko ya ka ye nngwe
yeo e hlokometsego mathatana a yona
ge ke hlohletsa ka maleng a marokgo
go tswa masela a dipotla feela
ka maswabi ke leka momywanywo
le agee ntate
momywanywo o thunya go tswa marung a maso
ao a okaokago sefahlego sa gagwe
ke a leboga ke mo kwa a realo
e le ge ke hlabela pele
bodibeng bja pelo yo ka go tletse senthulane
sa kganyogo ya go tsetsemetsa

* Phaswane's Sepedi adaptation of 'Time To Rest'.

kganyogo yeo e tsetsemetsago
ya go re ke bowe mo boruthong bja menywanywo
yeo e lwago le maru a maso
ao a swaraganego ka katlano
le meago ya malekeleke ya khonkhoriti ya hillbrow
le sa ikemetse gona fao leboto
le ge le se sa na mogagabo lona
aibo ke kwa pelo ya ka e goeletsa
e le ge dipono tsa mabitla
di kgeregela ditshika tsa ka tsa madi
gomme ge phiso ka ditshikeng
e nkgabakgabisetsa go tsogeng
ke ikana ka la gore ke a tseba
ke a tseba gore le thonkga pelo
leboto lela ge le ikemetse
ntle le monywanywo . . .

June 1998
Berea, Johannesburg

Our Braamfontein Hobos

there was this one clean
always with a red & white striped blanket
slung over his shoulder
& trailing behind him
we did not bother to ask for his name
or where he came from
but then he also kept silent
when we greeted him
looking at us with glassy eyes
eyes that gave us elusive signals
certainly not anger
but then no desire to belong to the community
of talking human beings
he was clean & organised every time
he would go to our neighbouring hillbrow
but we knew at five or six in the evening
he would be there
there at the wall of the wits university
in jan smuts avenue
digging into rubbish bins for his supper
& later spreading his blanket
on the cement floor
carving a path for his tired bones & flesh
to get to the lands of the gods
where they would be stretched & rested
we loved this man
our braamfontein hobo
who was too busy with life
too busy to be bothered
by insignificant details like us

but they were not all like him
another one was there too
with bushy hair milling with lice
& other creatures
probably not having washed for a decade
we would find him every breakfast time
further down from our braamfontein man
his fingers searching for lice
in his displayed pubic hair
with the testicles dangling
in their dark skin bag
the penis doing its customary dangle dance
he too never greeted us
being too busy with life
to see insignificant details

but we said silently
may the gods be with him too
for we knew
we knew with those words
we were praying for hobos
trying to lull into sleep
hobos of all shades
doing their rounds
in the depths of our hearts

(Undated)

HIV Nights

we called them gumbas
our friday night parties
we ate & drank with our mouths
& bottoms too
the beers the brandies the food
then in the early hours of the morning
we carried the gumbas to our student rooms
where we gulped
steaming semen & vaginal juices
thus we killed friday nights
& our dreams
we drowned our dreams
in oceans of alcohol
& baked them away
in the heat of the mornings
there could be no cooler breaks
from the burden of books
the disappointing grades
the markers' corrosive comments
until the doctors looked us gravely in the eye
& said
but children it's too late now
we still do not have a cure

(Undated)

Elegy For The Trio

i saw heard things
as i lay in the blanket
of night
my eyes piercing through the roof
watching twinkling stars
i heard the wind howling
jackals too
& the hooting of owls
the sounds of night
awakened the night of my heart
echoes of thabo manto mokaba[1]
haunted the hall of my skull
drugs drugged
the west tore nkosi[2] apart
& devoured parks[3]
hiv does not cause aids
but let thy condom come
anyway
the fear the flame continued
my body blackened
like a charred coal

1. President Thabo Mbeki, Health Minister Manto Tshabalala-Msimang, and the late Peter Mokaba, leader of the ANC Youth League, whose 'denialist' stances on the link between HIV and AIDS, and the use of anti-retroviral drugs, caused much controversy.
2. Nkosi Johnson, born HIV positive to a black mother and fostered by a white woman. He died at the age of twelve (see Glossary, p. 210).
3. Parks Mankahlana, President Mbeki's spokesperson, who died in October 2000 from, it is widely suspected, AIDS-related complications.

as i lulled myself back into sleep
i heard the echoes scream
my dreams into nightmares
i turned grey & cold like ash
no test tomorrow
i said again

(Undated)

*love*Life

the only roll-on every woman wants
the billboards say
& we say . . .
we are not that woman

now that they say you are positive
bone of my heart
i will write you this *love*Letter

i am waiting for words to run
to the tips of my fingers
but they enjoy the warmth
in the heart of my heart
feeding on the placenta
of my dreams for tomorrow

silence too is love
bone of my heart
let us lie on the green
& bask

(Undated)

Jude The Obscure[1]

snowy evenings of oxford streets
challenge us to a duet
we arm ourselves with layers
of t-shirts & skippers & shirts
& jerseys & coats & woolly gloves
& hats that hide our chilled ears
we move . . . wade through the nights
to the madding crowds of *jude the obscure*
& we say had the oxford
university press
had a taste for rhymes
& rhythms it would follow our trails
to thomas hardy's theatre
where *jude* strides naked across the stage
of lines bringing warmth & sad memories
to the expectant hearts of masses
savouring snowy foams of guinness
with hairs twitching excitedly from the mouths
of their eager noses & tongues
rollicking out sweet words of reverence
for the taste of blackness
& whiteness colouring glasses
that zigzag through this milling
of guinness-infested crowds
i let my eyes wander on to the wall paintings
to see the importance of being earnest

1. *Jude the Obscure* is the name of a pub in Oxford, not far from Oxford University Press.

underlying the presence of oxford brookes[2]
students who fled the noisy laughter
of their younger companions
those sweet under-sixteens swaying their hips
at *morals*[3] & calling it a break
but oh sweet *jude* . . .
jude your drums & poetry leave my homesick
memories to drift in
& out of *sweeney's*[4]
i dream of bringing the poetry
& drum culture of your walls
to the braamfontein centre
where witsies[5] could gather on wednesday evenings
to drown their sorrows in torrents
of castle lager or stand the test of time
of anxious parents in the sweet waves
of charles glass's[6] swimming pool
come *jude* . . .
i embrace your seduction warmly
neither sinful nor quite obscure
it drives students away from the dangerous
& lovely gleam of hillbrow lights
or that corner of *morals* where a girl
sucks the cork of an amused boy

2. Refers to Oxford Brookes University in Oxford, where Phaswane studied in 1997.
3. *Morals* is a student pub at Morrell Hall, Oxford Brookes University.
4. Now closed, *Sweeney's* was a pub situated in the Braamfontein Centre, opposite the University of the Witwatersrand in Johannesburg.
5. Students of the University of the Witwatersrand.
6. Charles Glass founded Castle Lager, a South African lager, in 1895.

who in turn digs his tongue into the mouths
of other girls forming a circle of friendship
while his companion stares at him
with widening eyes & salivating mouth
awaiting his share of the underwaist bliss
jude your walls bathe us with wisdom
of elders cherishing rhymes
& rhythms of life lived in our days
& with that wisdom i sing
& beat drums to salute you
my computer leaves strokes of lines
immortalising *morals* experiences
& wondering if those are freedom
breezes blowing in the land of learning
but i also cry . . .
i cry *jude* . . .
jude i cry for those rhythms of your warmth
that i left behind in the vicinity of snowy nights
& layers of clothing peeling off
to expose your beauty
i cry for you
& for *sweeney's* that is no more

July 1998
Berea, Johannesburg

The Going

i am a mountain
tumbling down
from great heights
to meet you
& sing when mandela
goes
i'll crush under the burden
of his history
& drown in the pool
of his shadow
i'll wail
for mellow
days
of brutal tales
swept under the carpet
by agents of truth
suddenly sighting
eruptions of the horror
of their love
enveloping them
& i'll reconcile
with the flag in hand
& atomic bombs
exploding in the pit
of jo'burg
i'll sing tales of woe
write memoirs of the old man
with the sweat
of half-ripe reconciliation
hanging from its tree

i'll cry
in tongues
& laugh with notes
of freedom
for i shall live
& follow
when
he takes
his rest

April 1998
Berea, Johannesburg

Mosepelo*

ke thaba
ke labile fase
go tswa magodimong a godimodimo
go tla go kopana nago
re opele ge mandela
a sepela . . .
ke tla thubega ka fase go morwalo
wa bophelo bja gagwe
gomme ka kgamega ka bodibeng
bja moriti wa gagwe
ke tla goeletsa ke llela
matsatsi a mabosana
a dikanegelo tse disoro
tseo di fsieletswego
ka fase ga khapete
ke badirela nnete
ge ka pejana ba bona
phulego ya mahlomola
a lerato la bona
a ba tatetsa
ke tla boelana le batho
ka folaga ka seatleng
le dipomo tsa athomo
di ththupa ka mpeng
ya jo'burg
ke tla opela dikanegelo tsa masetlapelo

* Phaswane's Sepedi adaptation of 'The Going'.

ka ngwala megopolo ya tsa bophelo bja motala
ka sethitho
sa poelano ya go se felele
yeo e tekeletsego mohlareng wa yona
ke tla lla
ka maleme a sele
ka sega ka legowa
la tokologo
gobane ke tla phela
gomme ka latela
ge a itseela
maikhutso
a gagwe

June 1998
Berea, Johannesburg

Freedom, Love & Songs

you're the ember
bringing warmth to chilled memories
of bloodfilled streets
of sharpeville & other villes
& roaring students' amandlas of '76
you're sunrays
throwing chunks of light
into turbulent hearts
sawing chains of entrapment
within brooding days of unrequited love
you're today
raising questions about tomorrow
wondering when mandela goes . . .
freedom day
you're . . .
you're joyful memories of yesterday
splattered across my chest
pains of betrayal lurking beneath the skin
of truth & reconciliation
you're anxiety
repressed by political correctness
& relevance of rainbowism
love
you come & retreat
retreat & come . . .
you torment my soul
with your teasing smile
hope mingles with blood
of angry vengeance
of cold thoughts of tomorrow's voices

shouting
but are you . . .
are you angels of african renaissance
turning round & round in the wombs
of mfecane
you're . . .
you're . . .
you're . . .
you're the bone of my heart
oozing with the marrow
of possible memories of tomorrow

April 1998
Berea, Johannesburg

Dikosa Tsa Tokologo Tsa Lerato*

o legala o tlisa
borutho megopolong ya go kgahla
ya diterata tsa go tlala madi
tsa sharpeville le di-ville tse dingwe
le legowa la amandla la baithuti
ba '76
o mahlasedi a letsatsi
ao a beletsago makwate a seetsa
dipelong tsa leemaema la matshwenyego
ao a segago diketwane tsa melaba
matsatsing a maso
a lerato la go se nwe a mokgako
o lehono
ge le tsosa dipotsiso ka gosasa
o makala gore
ge mandela a sepela . . .
letsatsi la tokologo
o . . .
o megopolo ya lethabo
ya maabane yeo e ikgasitsego
sehubeng sa ka
mahloko a keko a patlame ka fase ga letlalo
la nnete le poelano
o matshwenyego
a go gatelelwa ke phefolo ya dipolitiki
le maswanedi

* Phaswane's Sepedi adaptation of 'Freedom, Love & Songs'.

a bolalatladi
lerato la ka
o tla o goma
o goma o etla . . .
o hlorisa moya wa ka
ka monywanywo wa gago wa kaelano
tshepo e dubagana
le madi
a boitefeletso bja pefelo e soro
menagano yeo e tsidifetsego
ya mantsu a ka moso
ge a goeletsa
a re a . . .
a le mangeloi
a african renaissance
ao a phethogaphethogago
ka popelong
ya mfecane
letsasi la tokologo
o . . .
o . . .
o . . .
o lerapo la pelo ya ka
leo le tshotshomago ka mmoko
wa kgonagalo ya megopolo
ya ka moso

June 1998
Berea, Johannesburg

Women, Love & Songs, 1956

we threw the pass in
& with the dompas weighing heavily
the wheelbarrow trudged on
its iron wheel grinding discrimination
against the tarred roads
to union buildings
we sang & cried
& threw clenched fists into the air
& barry hertzog turned round
& round in the coffined womb
of his racialised renaissance
where sol plaatje & herbert dhlomo
would die screaming in the horrors
of urban areas act
& drowning in the bile
of population registration act
we sang & wheeled it on
to bring the african renaissance
well into the nineties
& now we sing with hoarse voices
we sing of freedom that hides
beneath the mask of equality
we sing of african renaissance
& shudder at the red oceans
of mfecane's aftermath
flowing into the rainbowism
of the richmond existence

& soapy floods of serial rapists'
fleshy guns gushing their way
through the supple thighs
of our east rand

August 1998
Berea, Johannesburg

Youth, Love & Songs

who do they say you're
yes they say it
say you're . . .
you're memories
of hector peterson
groaning between the teeth
of roaring floods
of cops' bullets
you're a stage toward
the african renaissance
of charles mungoshi beating
his own drum
with peterson singing blues
to the sonorous beat
while waiting for showers
from those brooding clouds
freedom day . . .
you're afrikaans declared
the official tongue
amidst clatters of multilingualism
& multiculturalism kissing the idea
of rainbowism welcome
& multibudgetism wandering
in the north with ngoako ramatlhodi
wondering about the youth now
that trevor manuel has cried foul
has bemoaned the drought
stalking the lands of national budgets
for school books
youth day . . .
you're memories of pain
of those bygone years

now bathing in these turbulent days
of equality spelt with notes
of outcomes & 2005
you're the turbulence
of african language publishing
translating the renaissance into obet
& humming notes of hope
in the face of english & science
riding high on the waves
of government concern
you're youth çensored
for scribbling lines in african languages
in praise of freedom
of freedom that zigzags its way through
the casualties of constitutionality
you're the youth accused of vulgarism
by the apartheid backbone
of language boards
spilling over into the rainbow
of today's dreams
a euphemism here . . . there child
substituting moralism for morality
& you'll find your way
into the school market
where your peers are caught
blowing up the guilds
of received wisdom of language equity
oh youth day . . .
you make me scream
cry for the freedom that i have
being raped by the repression that was
you're today . . . freedom day
waking up to the meaning of freedom
you're sibusiso bengu
& mary metcalfe backing up stimela's blues

see the world through the eyes of a child . . .
you're the child wondering
whether you still have eyes
to lead you into the dream of renaissance
when authorities' visions of your freedom
are a menace castrating your creative future
youth day . . .
you're a hen brooding over her eggs
haunted by the nightmare of decaying smell
of some dead eggs
with eardrums jarred by the live ones
screaming for independence
wanting to warm themselves up
in the rays of the beaming autumn ember
straddling these blue heavens with grim victory
& jog their memories through the cool showers
blessing the land in moments of confusion
bone of my heart . . .
say again . . . who do they say
you're . . .
yes they say it
but you sit there quietly with searing pain
embracing the deep joy encased
within the bone of your heart
knowing what it means
to beat your own drum
in the heart of blinding beams
of starving bullets
rattling their bones in the rifles
of baffled angels
that guard this kraal of our artistry . . .

June 1998
Berea, Johannesburg

Half-A-Crown Memory Lane
(On Nelson Mandela's 80th birthday)

i am the hoary octogenarian
the offspring of plaatje's mating
with shakespeare & oral history
of khunwana massacre
& the mfecane aftermath
they said what would happen
when publishers reject me
& i smiled . . .
i cried at the shortsightedness of their visions
& the shortness of their memories
for father created me long before he built me
the narrative shelter
he had already cleared the grounds by 1912
but we did not call those grounds
of african renaissance the anc then . . . no no . . .
we thought the sannc left no ugly stain
on the white sheets of our stressful existence
so i steered the sannc from behind closed doors
while i lived on in the air of the land
in the chilly waters of the union . . .
until my existence exploded into the public
arena of clattering curiosity of the early 1930s
clement doke thought my existence
should have been in setswana
& i said it would be as is & was
in setswana & the spirit of multilingualism
i split myself into fiction
& journalism & politics . . .
i said yes . . .
why not baptise one piece nelson mandela

but the renaming confused many
they mistook me for a newborn baby
who is now a hoary octogenarian
trumpeting the story of the coming
of rainbowism from houghton mansions
where i adorn his bookshelves
& flow through his thoughts
of a better tomorrow
& build bridges to carry
us into the flourishing
of local fictions & rhythms
where stories lose nothing by repetition . . .

July 1998
Berea, Johannesburg

An Ode To Bafana Bafana

ai
we sang . . .
we sang shosholoza
sent you off with rhymes
of joy & hope stifled
by our knowledge of your youth
in matters of world cups
we brooded over the deprivations
& depravities of apartheid
of amabokoboko
beating ireland with scores
of fists that frightened the irish
made them fearful
of scoring their own goals
to fill oceans of nationhood
flowing within their literature
james joyce forgot about the artist
as a young man
& focused his sharp gaze
on you bafana bafana
playing your first round like boys
stranded in a zoo
of noisy spectators screaming au revoir
benny mccarthy magic
& no wonder boys
there was no madiba magic
spurring you on from the maddening crowds
of noises of shosholoza
uprooted from its south african soil
& stranded in the green lands

of bastille letting you
eat cake in the days
of cocked starvation stalking your feet
bafana bafana you lost
you lost amidst clatters of xenophobia
corroding the guts of philippe troussier
& the xenophobes joining
nigerians in hillbrow streets
chanting when the super eagles
bliksem the brazilians
the south & the west of africa will flow
into each other
& together march onward
to take america captive
& iraq caught these whiffs
of colonialism reincarnated
who knew that iraq could sing so
it sang its voices hoarse
screaming of the african renaissance
spreading itself through american soccer fields
& hollywood movies
taking shelter under trembling shadows
of big screens while kwaito
rhythms beat their ways
through african cinemas
& victims rolling diseased phlegm
around their receptive tongues
& with gusto hurling it at fellow victims
iraq wondered at them that so spat
in the face of soccer mania
haunting the saudi arabian coach
losing his bread
first it was buttered on both sides

& on the edges too
& then before he could take a bite
the edges were knifed off
before his gaping mouth
& he guided his eyes
through the baffled air
toward the fingers that he would lick
but they too found that the sides
were merely mirages of butter
that melted in the heat
of the battlefield
america laughed at us
until put to a shameful death
& now they roll in the grave
their ghosts wandering in the valleys of iraq
& wondering in the depths
of warfare turned world cup
scandal amidst the english hooligans
menacing their way
into the jungle of saudi arabian fans
you lost bafana bafana
but we knew you were stimela's franky
wanting to go to the city
it is enticing & menacing that hillbrow
that you would go to
softly now boys . . .
tread softly as you wade your way
toward 2002
a big leap toward 2006 and beyond
when we might watch from heavens
as you soar like eagles
pursuing xenophobia
& leaving hillbrow

with hovering clouds
of spotless cleanliness
blending with brooding darkness
of multiforked rainbowism

July 1998
Berea, Johannesburg

From Our Hillbrow Tower

we will get those terrorists
they said
they did

they struck at the world trade centre
& the pentagon
fragments of civilisation came tumbling down
we've always seen it in the movies
but it was bigger more spectacular
this knifed explosion of civilisation
we were shocked into silence & awe
we marvelled at the advanced civilisation
of photography capturing the moment
perhaps it was like a dream a nightmare
in which we'll continue to live
perhaps it's a dream an apparition
this superpower groaning
& bellowing like an ox being castrated
squealing like a pig hit with a heavy knobkerrie
between its eyes that twinkle with fear

we cry with you america
we said from our hillbrow
but who knows who's wrong
who knows that anyone's right
has america not always terrorised the world
thus other echoes from the pit of our hillbrow

hosanna bin laden
alleluia
bring us liberation

we will get those folks
they sent the message through the airwaves
bring him alive or dead
taliban bring him out
before we smoke you out of your terrorist caves
grab you by the scarves of your necks
& drag you across the atlantic to our white house
to extract the truth nothing but the truth

they did get the folks in kandahar
& jalalabad
they did get the slow folks
babies children parents trapped in the forests
& valleys & caves of afghanistan
the quickfooted ones were blown into the skies
just as they crossed the borders of pakistan
& the bombs continued to smoke
all out of their caves of terror & innocence

still bush said we demand him
that longbearded man
with a head wrapped in a woman's headcloth
that apparition in white
screaming calls against our civilisation
give him no voice
you voices of america & the world
kill the freedom of the voice
that we fought for
for centuries
these are strange times indeed
only talk of the sweet milk
flowing from the mouths of bushes
we live in strange times

the strikes against terror
went on snubbing out the buds of innocence
still america said we're getting there
soon very soon
blame it all on the taliban
if we don't

but we wondered if osama
was not the slender shaved man
we met in *the voice* the other night
wrapped in warm blankets
treating himself to a cold south african lager
& singing praise allah
singing much louder than our kwaito rhythms
& listening to the cnn gossips & rumours
of the strikes against terror
in the far north
& smiling at america's deafness
to the world's calls for love
& compassion
calls against the spilling of innocent blood

he was there this man
smiling
saying america has brains of a donkey
for don't we know that fools
can dish you out as delicacy during breakfast
& lunch & supper
simply because they've the muscle
to smash your body against rocky mountains

& the bombs continued to explode
we live in strange times

our hearts reach out to you
america of milk & honey & bile
our hearts reach out to you too
afghanistan of sweet & bitter streams
flowing down your mountain slopes
& snaking their ways through your forests
& bulrushes
& bushes

our hearts' reach digs
deep into the recesses of our hillbrow
in which we drink muddied news
of the strikes against terror
we vomit streams of smoked blood
tributaries of our new consciousness
we're constipated by tons
of roasting corpses filling the caves
of tora bora
these are strange times indeed

we too swear we're in this war against terror
if only we could find it
this terror hidden somewhere
locked far away in the dark chambers
of our ruffled hearts

(Undated)

God Doesn't Smoke Dagga

God Doesn't Smoke Dagga

I was asleep, not quite. You may call it a dream. I don't know what to call it. Do we dream even when we are awake, not quite; but not quite asleep, either? It was in this strange space between sleep and non-sleep, the attempt at sleep and the simultaneous attempt at remaining awake, trying to think through what I had heard at the Johannesburg Hospital earlier in the day that this picture of Lesedi visited me. It was by now a familiar picture. I have seen it often. We had spent many nights and dawns at each other's flats, in each other's beds, arms, mouths and the southern hemispheres.

I looked at the picture that Lesedi had drawn.

A portrait of Braamfontein, she told me.

It could not have been obvious to anyone unfamiliar with this suburb what she was up to. Even I, who had spent nearly fifteen years here – as a student and a resident – could not fathom what the portrait could have stood for. Perhaps it was the rough manner in which she did it. No one doubted that she could have drawn a much better picture, if precision and accuracy could be said to be the most desirable features of an artwork. She had drawn pictures with utmost precision and accuracy before. What is more, she had added colour to them; different shades that enabled anyone to see that this was the inner-city Johannesburg, Jozi; that, Braamfontein; and that over there, Hillbrow. Buildings stood out recognisably. But this time round – for the first time since her university studies in Art, she told me – she chose to make only a rough portrait. And what perhaps made it particularly difficult for me to make out my familiar Braamfontein on it was what formed the background to the suburb. For my mind had wandered to the background; once there, it refused, against my wishes, to explore the whole portrait.

In this background of Lesedi's Braamfontein was a huge, but rather faintly drawn, image of what initially looked like an old man, with a large bunch of kinky hair that was separated in the middle by a generous supply of baldness. I had to look at the picture closely.

You're so obsessed with detail, Lesedi had said, when I lifted the huge picture from the wall, so that I could look at it more closely.

Details. The stuff of life. I remembered what Dr Legora had said in the first writing workshop I attended a couple of years ago. God lives in the details.

We all know oranges? Dr Legora had asked. Of course! we had shouted back with enthusiasm, most of us, no doubt, hiding our puzzlement at such a pointlessly rhetorical question.

Write me a description of an orange, he had said. That is going to be the basis of stories that we are going to write for homework, which we will share tomorrow.

We set to work on this piece of work. First things first: the most notable thing about oranges is that they are orange. We all talked about that colour. We nearly all ventured to talk about their taste, although our descriptions of this varied. Then, some wrote about their class: citrus fruit. Someone who knew a bit about the medicinal value of oranges talked about them as a great fountain of Vitamin C, which boosted the human immune system, that strengthened the body's soldiers, as we would say; although, having read this in a recent issue of the *Mail & Guardian*, our classmate pointed out that *marula* might be an even better source of health. The piece she referred to was an article on the *marula* fruit, which grew largely in Limpopo, and which medical scientists were considering as a possible future ingredient of immunity boosters, especially with a view to using them to depress the rapid development, growth and spread of the HI viruses in the body.

Dr Legora had then teased us on the obvious: the colour of oranges. He had taken an orange out of his coat pocket, peeled the skin off with his hands – no knife. Now, he said again, we all know oranges? Our responses refracted.

The colour of oranges. The God of detail, the detail in God, the details of God . . .

I had continued to examine Lesedi's portrait of the old man with kinky hair. He had a large pipe in his right hand, again faintly drawn – more faintly than the picture of the old man himself. But the pipe was almost as big as the man's head. Smoke drifted its way from the pipe into the air. I then examined the facial features of the man. Something fascinated me there. Lesedi had to some extent reproduced the picture of God that she had bought when she first came to do her degree of Bachelor of Arts in Fine Art at the University of the Witwatersrand, or Wits. She was a Christian, then; a church-going Christian.

I stopped going to church because, she would tell me later, people don't pray with their hearts.

They prayed, yes. Their eyes closed, their mouths shouting out words to the Almighty, and their hearts empty of any thought as to what their words meant. Priests promising their flocks that they could cure AIDS with their prayers and holy waters, and in the process encouraging, cajoling their diseased flocks into forking out their last cents to buy this sacred cure. The great servants of the Lord dribbling their flocks with knowledgeable words of the mysterious, the heavenly. God's cure descending to the Earth, in a chariot, at costs that left the pockets of the congregations full of holes. Lesedi stopped going to church because people were not religious, spiritual.

Church, God, is in me, she said with finality.

So she worshipped her God in silence, and used this particular picture of God on her wall as a template through which to think of her own God; of her Gods of the Arts, and the Arts of the Gods. There were things I could not have known, then. Things she could not have known, either. Both of us comfortable knowing, as we did, our humble paths through life. Until, one day, after a lengthy conversation, we yielded to the Call. A Call that many people were not prepared to heed.

The God that Lesedi had bought was a white God, with fairly short-cropped, but visibly curly hair. His hands did not hold any pipe; they clasped within them the hands of his Angels, clearly singing with abandon. In the far distance I could see dark figures with horns and forks in their hands, their backs turned against the singing, although they looked over their shoulders to see what God and his Angels could be up to. Flames of fire obscured these shady figures somewhat.

I recall these figures only too well. Not just because they were on the picture that the then church-going Lesedi had bought. I remember them, too, because when I read Herman Charles Bosman's story, 'Unto Dust', I could not help feeling that the angels with cloven hoofs and forks that his character, Stoffel Oosthuizen, saw as he lay dying – the Angels he saw because of his stainless path through the joys and tribulations of life, he told his fellow Boers – could only have been drawn from a picture such as Lesedi's. It was a familiar picture in all civilised, Christian households.

But, as I said, the God of Lesedi's handiwork was black, although with facial features that closely resembled those of the white God that she had bought.

I asked her to explain the significance of her drawing. She refused.

Art is something you experience. What it means to you, it means, she told me.

I pondered this, trying to understand her words, reflecting on her portrait. My attendance at the writing workshops had not resulted in my writing anything. No poem, no story. I was just like the many other people who believed that they had poems, novels, in them. Works that never ventured into the warmth and cold of our universe. I suppose that I feared my prospective critics, doubted my abilities. After all, I was not sure that I understood artwork. Perhaps that is why I wished she could explain hers to me.

Again I pondered her words, reflected on her portrait. I remembered the popular expression in our rural village of Tiragalong, near Polokwane.

God doesn't smoke dagga, we used to, we still, say.

Could Lesedi be playing on this expression? It was the kind of expression that we uttered when someone was in trouble; it meant that God would look after them, deliver them from the storms of life, and rid them of the ways of the shady figures, such as were reflected in Lesedi's portrait.

God doesn't smoke dagga.

I walked out of my sleep, into wakefulness. Strolled to the kitchen, poured a beer mug full of tap water. Strolled back into the bedroom of my Braamfontein flat. I did not head for the bed, though. The balcony beckoned; I accepted its invitation. I faced the glowing blue lights of the newly opened Nelson Mandela Bridge. Beautiful by night, not so impressive by day. The advertisements for the looming erection of the bridge were far more spectacular, more impressive to the mind than this dwarf of a bridge. Great expectations carefully watered, well grown, and now colliding with the cruel reality of the structure itself. It was the bridge that ran from the end of Bertha Street – across the dreary railway tracks that took you into Park Station and beyond – to the renovated cultural precinct of Newtown, where the famous Market Theatre was, is. In the day, you stood on the bridge and saw nothing, nothing pleasantly impressive or gentle to the eye. To the north was Braamfontein, a suburb as quiet and dull as Hillbrow is vibrant, exciting and scary, at least to some people. To the east was Hillbrow itself; tall, unattractive buildings that were peeling off and collapsing like a piece of shit attacked by dung beetles. Hillbrow stood hand in hand with Joubert Park and the city centre, which in turn stood hand in hand with Hillbrow. A triangle of mess, excitement. It was this triangle that the Mandela Bridge was intended to help the wealthy from the northern suburbs – the supposedly angelic workers and students resident in Braamfontein, Wits academics, and, of course, tourists – to dodge on their way to the Market Theatre in Newtown. The inner city was made up of Newtown and the rest of the inner city areas, the Jozi of street vendors and thugs crashing into cars at the robots, in pursuit of wallets, purses and cellphones. Now, it was possible to skirt round the grime and crime, to forget the dirty street kids and hobos, the working and lower middle classes, the students resident in the triangle of mess and excitement, all the locals and Makwerekwere of our City of Gold and Dust. For now, all of this was possible.

In His, Mandela's, Honour . . .

I might have been tempted to walk up to the top of the Bridge, for lack of anything else to do, were it not midnight already. So instead I switched on my CD player. I listened to Kenny Rogers playing *Ruby Don't Take Your Love to Town*. A song about a crippled man in a war, whose wife deserts him at dusk, every day, taking her bodily rubies elsewhere. A song of love betrayed. *And if I could move I would take my gun and put her underground*, the crippled man said, with much nostalgia for the juicy old days, the deep sadness and resentment for the present, and the despair for tomorrow. I walked back into the bedroom to feed my ears with more of this bomb of a song. I wondered what Kenny Rogers could have seen that made him sing such a beautifully despairing and depressing piece.

I knew I was not going to take any gun; no need, in this Braamfontein of ours, to put anyone underground. No need that I could think of straight away. Except that a gunshot in the streets disturbed my train of thought. Nothing unusual in that, if you live in Jozi.

God doesn't smoke dagga . . .

I must have been asleep, with the gun to put Ruby underground still playing. I recalled my dream, my nightmare. Two plates lying in front of me, one full of sex and sex, the other full of love and sex. This second plate floated into the air, blowing about like a balloon, and disappearing like a foam bubble in a strong wind, like a balloon that drifted its way into a thorn tree, as soon as I reached out for it. I followed the plateful of love and sex as it kept on reappearing with the other one as soon as I had given up on it. The two floated their way into the street, which was Bertha Street. They floated past Wits, southbound. We marched our way across Jorissen Street, then De Korte, Juta, Smit and, finally, Wolmarans. We used the Mandela Bridge to avoid the madding crowds of Hillbrow and Joubert Park and the inner city, heading for Newtown. We did not go to the Market Theatre, though. We entered the Horror Café, that place where artists and art lovers and supporters took tourists and their guests for meals and a drink. It was just a couple of streets away from the Market Theatre.

That is where Lesedi and I went for lunch when we first met in Jozi. We were a homeboy and homegirl on the verge of doing our thing in the city.

It was as we – I and my platefuls as companions – entered the Horror Café that I came to, that I walked out of my sleep. Ruby was still taking her love to town, in the CD player. I immediately thought about Lesedi at her University residence, wondered what she could be doing. I could have given her a call. Only, I had no cellphone. The Hillbrow vultures had usurped my first, expensive phone; the Joubert Park hyenas the second, cheaper one; and the third, the cheapest on the market, was appropriated in the inner city of surveillance cameras that did not appear to have been installed to protect those who, like me and my Lesedi, drove on the soles of our shoes. After this third occasion, I resolved not to own such accessories any more. This, even though I was aware that there was nothing, no strategy, that could evade appropriation in this city of ours.

I ran down the flight of stairs to the ground floor, to the coin phone booth down there. I picked up the handset. No coins in my pockets. I went back up to the flat. No coins there, either; just a stack of notes that would be of no use under the circumstances. My mind wandered.

I reflected again on Lesedi's portrait of God.

The feeling that surged from my innermost being as I trudged my way back to the duvet, the comforter, was one of burning; not like fire, not like anything I knew, really. It was a feeling that I was experiencing for the first time. I began to sweat. My hair stood on end, ready to fly. Was this what people felt when they were possessed by the Spirit of Satan, and of God, I wondered? I sweated streams of heat, of confusion. What could I have said to Lesedi, had I had those coins? I had kept silent when the nurse at Johannesburg Hospital talked to us. I wished she could have talked with us instead. I suspected we understood such things much better than she did. What could I have said, then? What rang through my head, as I entered the Hospital, was that Jozi's sick.

Johannesburg's sick; Lesedi had voiced this before I could, right there, at the reception. The crowds of sick people milling like bees in a hive . . . The understaffed Hospital that gave you an appointment for four or five weeks time, even as the nurses and doctors agreed that your case was urgent.

Jozi's sick, I thought, jumping out of bed. I went downstairs again, walked past our night security guard who was always fast asleep in his glass cabin, smelling of brandy. I had often asked myself why Dunwell Properties, the owners of this, and most other Braamfontein residential blocks, tolerated his conduct: making it his business to drink and sleep at work. I opened the security door. Although there was a note saying our security depended on our locking this door, we never actually received any keys to it, and the security guard never locked it. Our security depended on his two mutual companions: Brandy and Sleep. I opened the never-locked door. I turned left and directed my feet to Lesedi's residence. I knew that Wits Security would probably not let me in, at that early hour of the morning. But I went there all the same.

What's wrong with Lesedi? asked one of the two security officers, who knew me quite well. We had had a chat many times. Lesedi, being such a pleasant soul, was also a good friend of his. He had always told me how different she was from the rest, or at least most, of the girls in the residence; she was the kind of woman who did not run after the stick in every pair of trousers, or the wheels that they rode on, or even the credit cards that those trousers carried in their pockets. He had noticed, as Lesedi came back from the Hospital the previous morning – for he was working a double shift then – that all was not so well with her; that there was a cloud of brooding hovering around her face. But she had declined to say what the matter was.

As he asked me the question, a thought struck me.

Secrecy, too, could be a source of strength. So I said: I, too, am in the dark.

As it turned out, Lesedi was not sleeping, the officer said. She was watching TV. Alone in the communal TV room, although she had her own, much bigger and brighter TV set in her room. She had probably discovered the claustrophobia of smaller and closed spaces. She was alone. At three in the morning. So he went up to the first floor to check if she was willing to see me.

We walked back to my flat, I and Lesedi; to the flat where we would lie down in silence. There was much to discuss. But for now silence would do.

When the nurse, the counsellor, let the news out, I had not remained silent. When I said earlier that I remained silent, what I meant was that she could not have understood me. I had to be with Lesedi, to make certain that she, unlike the nurse, the counsellor, understood. Through silence initially. Through words later, if need be.

If I could find the words. I wanted her to understand that I had no thought, no intention whatever, of taking any gun to put her underground. She had wondered earlier, at the Hospital, before we saw the counsellor, where this thing could have come from. I wanted her to understand that there was no point, there could be no point in trying to dig out the roots. Sex and sex; love and sex; compassion, kindness, generosity and blood donations; the blood tests when the doctors tried to understand her earlier ailments; injections, needles . . . Who could know where the roots lay?

So, as we lay under the comforter, we kissed many kisses, embraced with many embraces. We did not talk. We shed, shared tears. Platefuls of tears of love and sex . . .

And as we did this, I kept on wondering, quietly:

But what, exactly, does God smoke . . . ?

Healing With Words: Phaswane Mpe Interviewed By Lizzy Attree*

Phaswane Mpe died suddenly on 12 December 2004, in Polokwane, South Africa, at the age of 34. This is one of the last interviews recorded with him. I had hoped to check accuracy with him, but he was taken from us too soon. I hope I have rendered all he said faithfully and am grateful to him for sparing the time to speak to me. He was a great source of encouragement and inspiration, to me and many other students, a kind and generous man, who experienced and achieved such a lot in his short life, and he will be sorely missed. He was one of South Africa's most promising new writers. He is survived by two young children.

LA: I want to ask you first about your novel *Welcome To Our Hillbrow*, I wonder why you chose the novel form and whether you felt that that was something that came naturally or did you have to force it into that form? You said in the book that the short story seemed too short for the ideas that you wanted to explore. Is that part of the reason?

PM: It's a difficult one to answer. In the first place I didn't sit down and reflect on whether to choose the short story form or the novel form. I actually started it, as I was writing I simply thought I was doing a portrait of Hillbrow and portrayed it in a very geographical sense. And I actually thought I was just doing Hillbrow the map and that would be it. And as I came toward the end of the novel, I realized that I'm going to need a character to move around that map, so I thought back to my short stories and thought well in one moment I wrote a short story entitled 'Occasion for Brooding' and with that story that's when I first created the character of Refentše. As it would turn out, I had had Refentše commit suicide in that short story and in my moment of depression, when I started doing

* Lizzy Attree is a London-based writer, researcher and literature specialist. This interview first appeared in the *Journal of Commonwealth Literature*, 2005, 40 (3).

the Hillbrow map, I actually thought back to that character and thought I'm actually beginning to feel like my character. I'm going to try to cheer myself up by trying to resurrect him somehow, so I brought him into the novel. But as I say, as I was starting, it was just going to be that first chapter, but towards the end of the chapter I realized that there were things I could still address.

LA: And that chapter, still very much could stand alone, as a short story. Were you consciously trying to fill a gap that you felt people weren't writing about modern Hillbrow?

PM: Initially I wasn't trying to fill a gap. I wanted to do the map, simply out of depression I just wanted something to do and I actually started writing it very early on Sunday, in the morning, when I came to my office in the department of African literature to write an academic essay for a conference in Australia. But my mind just couldn't get to the academic essay, so I thought well, I can't go home. If I go home I don't know what I'm going to do, I have to do something so ja, it was almost like playing a game to cheer me up in my moment of depression.

LA: And this is drawn from your own experience of living in Johannesburg?

PM: Sure.

LA: How long have you lived in Johannesburg?

PM: I started living in Jo'burg from 1989 when I came to do my first year of Bachelor of Arts in the University.

LA: In the story there are elements which seem very autobiographical.

PM: Indeed.

LA: How autobiographical is it? I mean, the central character commits suicide . . .

PM: [laughs]

LA: You've talked about this depression and the way you needed to write this, to save yourself, somehow, or as a cure for something. How important do you think it is, as a cathartic form, to write and to produce creative work?

PM: What I say won't apply to everything I've written, in terms of creative writing. But certainly I wrote *Welcome To Our Hillbrow* with the purpose of keeping myself busy and in my case it worked extremely well. I locked myself in that office for the whole day and almost whole night. I left just before six o'clock in the morning, feeling very exhausted but absolutely thrilled that I'd done it. It would roughly have been about three-quarters of *Welcome To Our Hillbrow*, by the time I left the office. Ja, and then I spent five weeks working on about the last quarter of it. So it did work from that point of view. The other pieces of writing, short stories and poems, I wasn't writing with any therapeutic motives, I was simply thinking: here is an idea, let me see what I can do with an idea. So it was like entertaining myself, or whiling away the time, perhaps feeling bored. But I think we write for so many different reasons at different times and writing as therapy, in my case, would strictly apply to *Welcome To Our Hillbrow*, to that book and I would say to three poems I wrote on HIV/AIDS: one is published in that collection *Nobody Ever Said AIDS* [Kwela, 2004] and then there are two that got published. There's another one, '*love*Life', which got published in German translation, the English one has been rejected and then there's another one that has been rejected by the German journal, the people who published three of my poems and my very, very, very first story 'Brooding Clouds'. So, ja, I think just those three poems and the novel.

LA: If it's not too personal a question, can I ask what was the cause of the depression – is it living in Jo'burg?

PM: No, it wasn't living in Jo'burg. I won't be able to give you the details of what led to the depression, but it had a lot to do with very personal stuff that could have happened at home. It could have been anywhere. And certainly, I must say Jo'burg doesn't depress me, I like it.

LA: So in terms of the content, and the things that you wrote about, particularly AIDS, you deliberately chose those subjects, you had a reason to include them, is that right? You wrote the book out of a need to write, but you placed these ideas within the novel, there was a purpose in including them?

PM: I think if there is a purpose I would say it is embedded in just my desire to map Hillbrow, contemporary Hillbrow. Inevitably I think if you bring a character to move around you are not going to avoid the question of African Internationals in Hillbrow, that's one glaring presence. And along with that, would go the question of job creation and struggle over job opportunities. I didn't pursue that line, but I did mention it in passing. Another very important question would be the question of HIV/AIDS and prostitution. I didn't pursue prostitution as well, but I decided to pick up on HIV/AIDS because for me it linked very nicely with questions of xenophobia.

LA: It's notable that everyone in the novel dies . . .

PM: [laughs]

LA: Including the narrator, who is already dead. Does this reflect a form of pessimism or a lack of redemption that you see for these characters or is this just a device to round off their story?

PM: Many people have told me it is depressing, I wouldn't say it isn't, but I tend to think about it as one of the most optimistic [laughs] pieces of writing I've done.

LA: Because of the final character who comes back . . .

PM: Not just that, I think if you look at, I mean it's not just *Welcome To Our Hillbrow*, one could look at a range of texts where you have characters die but the portrayal of the characters and the nature of the plot is such that you look beyond the individual deaths of the characters. And I think that the vision, despite the obvious gloom that goes with death, the general vision I think is positive.

LA: OK. Both central characters write a form of fiction which they don't succeed in publishing. One character writes in English and one writes in Sepedi, what is your view on writing in Sepedi – did you translate *Welcome To Our Hillbrow* into Sepedi?

PM: I didn't translate it. I had a collection of short stories, which I translated into Sepedi. I experienced quite a number of problems with getting it published, but it was finally accepted for publication. The commissioning editor and I did not agree on how far to go with the editing. I felt at some point I was being censored, which I objected to. Nevertheless they said they would publish it, and at the end of the day it was not published. That's the *Brooding Clouds* collection. So some time in March 2002 I actually called the publisher to cancel our publishing contract. So I've got a typeset version of *Maru a Maso* which is the title I gave it.

LA: And what about the English version?

PM: The English version has been accepted by the publishers of *Welcome To Our Hillbrow* [UKZN Press]. We didn't publish it because we finally decided that I needed to do substantial changes which I never came round to doing.

LA: Is that revisions in the content? Or is that editorial?

PM: We identified gaps from one story to another. I needed to find ways of bridging those gaps. The problem I had with editorial questions, was simply in the Sepedi version of *Brooding Clouds*.

LA: But, in terms of using English as a form, you don't find that problematic?

PM: No I don't find that problematic. Do you want to take us to Ngugi? Let's just plunge into him [laughs].

LA: Especially in South Africa, it's actually a unifying form in some respects, it overrides divisions between races, which seems to be a positive reason to write in English.

PM: I think there is that positive reason to write in English, bridging the language gaps, but I think there is also something that is a purely practical consideration beyond that, which is that much of my instruction in school and university has been in English, so although I speak Sepedi much more fluently than I speak English – I'm actually used to writing in English. If I pick up my pen, the first thing I am going to do is to write in English. So it's that and I think because I am also sensitive to the language question. That's one of the reasons, in fact the main reason I translated the short-story collection. I didn't translate *Welcome To Our Hillbrow* because of my disappointment with the reception of the Sepedi collection. Ideally I would have done it a long time ago, even before I got the publisher of the English version. But I'm very aware that probably the first review I would get from a publisher would be that it is vulgar, if I translated it into Sepedi. And in as much as one appreciates one's language, you don't really want to waste time writing things that you know for sure you'll not get published. So I wouldn't be too sentimental about it.

LA: And does that relate also to audience? Do you think it reaches the audience that you would want?

PM: I think there are audiences that I am not reaching. I'm certainly reaching a significant audience by South African standards, which is to say not many people! But it seems to me that if I had an opportunity to, or if I had a very strong urge, and I decided to be very sentimental and got it published, if we were very lucky in Sepedi, I would also reach a certain audience that I wouldn't be able to reach in the English version. I know that, and it's a big problem in South Africa, in African indigenous languages we rely quite heavily on educational publishing. And if it were to be published and a publisher may present a good case to people who prescribe books, to committees that are selected to prescribe books to high schools, I would reach far more of an audience, the kind of audience that ultimately would not read *Welcome To Our Hillbrow*. So I actually think there's a big big big big audience that I'm not reaching and probably I'm never going to reach.

LA: Which ideally you would like to?

PM: Which ideally I would have liked to reach through translation.

LA: In that respect, you are being read in the United States and in Britain and particularly as a black author from the 'new' South Africa, your work has been significant in that sense, or at least it stands out especially to a Western audience as a successful transitional novel, post-apartheid period, particularly by a black author. Do you consider that your work forms part of a tradition, or do you see yourself as striking a new note in fiction in South Africa? Or do you follow on from someone else?

PM: Well, I think it is inevitable that one would fall into both camps. Partly forming part of a tradition and partly doing something different. As I re-read the novel, and indeed as I was writing, I would keep on thinking back to certain writers. Some of them I do mention in the novel, like Herman Charles Bosman. One could think of the likes of Zakes Mda, whom I also mention in the novel, while I don't discuss them of course – they only come up in passing, J.M. Coetzee, also mentioned, and of course one draws influence from the likes of Bessie Head, and of course I studied English literature, so Charles Dickens and Shakespeare and William Blake form part of my consciousness. Some of the authors in Sepedi like Oliver Matsepe, I use him as an epigraph at the beginning, so one borrows certain things from them. But also, I think issues like xenophobia and HIV/AIDS have not been discussed very much in South African literature written in English. So in that sense I think I'll be part of an emerging tradition, if you want to put it that way, which is of course not to overlook the fact that Afrikaans writers have been writing about HIV/AIDS – I can't read Afrikaans myself, but the name that keeps on coming up is Koos Prinsloo who started writing about HIV/AIDS from the 1980s. Ja, well he's been writing about HIV/AIDS from the early 1980s. He hasn't influenced my writing, but I'm aware and I think in some ways I'm following South African literature more broadly, not just in terms of English literature, you could say well, perhaps what

I'm doing is not part of a general tradition. But I think in South African literature in English, having xenophobia and HIV/AIDS treated in such a sensitive way is unusual.

LA: Have you noticed other fiction about HIV/AIDS from South Africa since you've written this novel?

PM: Well it seems to be popular in young adult teenage fiction. In what one might call middlebrow and highbrow literature, I've not seen it happening. It may well be that it is difficult to know what is getting published in South Africa as well. But I really think that one good example that happened for me was *Confessions of a Gambler*. I'm sorry I haven't come across any other adult novels dealing with the subject in a substantial way. It's mentioned in passing in nearly all significant novels.

LA: You can't avoid it in some respects. It was interesting that Rayda Jacobs chose that form of 'confession' to frame her novel. Do you think that need or that desire to name, or to talk about those subjects in South Africa, relates to a wider culture of speaking out? The TRC [Truth and Reconciliation Commission] has perhaps created a culture of speaking out, the title *Confessions of a Gambler* highlights the fine line between autobiography, biography and fiction and in comparison with Zimbabwe for example, where people don't discuss AIDS openly, it seems like a comparatively clear presence within South African literature? Is there a modern trend towards taboo breaking within art and literature, or is it a wider cultural trend?

PM: It seems to me that the literature of 'truth and confession', if one can put it that way, I think it is a rather narrow way of putting it, but maybe it will help me to answer the question, I think the literature of 'truth and confession' in South Africa has a very long history. I think that kind of history can be demonstrated by the number of autobiographies we've got here. I don't know, I might be exaggerating of course, but we probably have more autobiographies than any other African country.

It seems to me that that kind of literature has been with us for a long time. What seems to have happened is that in the 1990s the Truth and Reconciliation Commission provided an easy but perhaps problematic label for literature of 'truth and confession'.

LA: It's that need for storytelling as well, history being very public about private lives. It takes over; it was so widespread.

PM: It's very widespread but I actually think Es'kia Mphahlele made a fairly important point. He said in one of his writings that when he was writing *Down Second Avenue*, he would choose to highlight aspects of his personal life, that in many ways would be somewhat representative of the broader experiences of other black South Africans and I think that's generally what we have been having with South African autobiographies. I think what surprises me is why, as the Truth and Reconciliation Commission was giving impetus to new novels and I think it did, what surprises me is why HIV/AIDS did not feature so much in the TRC novels. While perhaps part of it might just be that the TRC was really not about disease, but it seems to me to be a very odd omission.

LA: Your book deals with very private individuals, they're not caricatures, they're not famous people. In a sense they're not particularly representative, they're students but they are relatively ordinary characters. Do you think this is part of what Achmat Dangor achieves in *Bitter Fruit*, this moving away from a very public sphere of life where these autobiographies come from, where people are heroes, or great politicians and feature in a historical context where they're part of the struggle? Do you think your novel is a move towards a more private, personal way of relating the world which doesn't deal with those bigger issues, it does, but not on the grand scale – is that quite deliberate on your part?

PM: Earlier on, I said that part of the novel is autobiographical and of course it is, and I think what the novel really reflects is the kind of circles I'm moving in. I don't feel I'm qualified to write about politics on a grand scale for example, because I don't spend much time with politicians and

I don't do much political research. So I don't think I've got the authority to speak on that grand scale and I accepted a long time ago that I'm leading a political life of some sort, on a small scale, and I think if that's what I can handle well, it's better to do something on a small scale and handle it well, than try to impress and fail to express oneself.

LA: To that end, in terms of books and literature generally, do you think there will be a time when this more personal, more stylistic, or aesthetic literature moves away from that politics, to a more art for art's sake idea, where people write because they are writers? It often comes up that African literature is connected with something political or the national struggle. To look at a more artistic basis for literature, do you think that's likely to happen?

PM: I think that's already happening. If one looks at *The Quiet Violence of Dreams* by Sello Duiker, I think he has done something very daring there by focusing that whole novel, and it's a huge novel, on homosexuality and black masculinities. It's not exactly what one might call a political novel in the way that people talk about political or historical novels. So I think that is already happening, perhaps on a small scale. But of course it is not art for art's sake. It's also grappling with politics of identity, which are crucial. So, perhaps a shorthand way of answering your question, I think there shouldn't necessarily be a tension between one's ideological/political/whatever endeavours, on one hand and an attempt to realize one's artistic skills on the other. So I think we'll always have people trying to develop their artistry as far as they can go, while of course propagating their ideas as much as they can, and I think it's a healthy combination. Ja, I would personally question people who say they are writing just for the sake of writing, I think there's always a motive, even if the motive is to say to those who say we must write with a political agenda, even if your motive is to say to them 'go to hell'. But I think there will be some motive.

LA: Sure. And then ultimately, is all of this a process of exploring the politics of identity, is it a process of self-definition in a new country where these stories have yet to be told? Is there a burden on the writer to tell these stories? Do you feel that impetus?

PM: I think of it not so much as a burden, but as an opportunity to explore stories that have not been told on the one hand and on the other, to revisit old stories, retell them in a new context and see what you can learn from the old stories. And perhaps also, in seeing what you can learn, in the process you'll also be seeing what you can retain and what you can do without in the present. I think in many ways then, one will always be dealing with a process of invention and revision and the processes will happen simultaneously.

LA: With that in mind, are you currently working on anything?

PM: No, I started very recently on something, I don't know what you call *Welcome To Our Hillbrow*, but something in that vein, semi-autobiography, semi-fiction. It's in the very early stages, I don't feel confident to talk about it, it's just, it's in such an early early stage.

LA: Is that connected with the story you read at the Wits Writing Centre recently?

PM: It's not connected with that story. I wrote that story, I was commissioned to write that story [*God Doesn't Smoke Dagga*] by New Africa Books. The story is published in *Urban 03*. That's the one I was reading at the Wits Writing Centre. In a collection called *Urban 03*.

LA: So, for the future, you're leaving WISER [Wits Institute for Social and Economic Research], switching your PhD to part-time, and you have decided to become a healer, is that right? What has led you in this new direction?

PM: Yes, I have decided to train as an Ngaka, which is the Sepedi term for healer. I will learn about herbal medicine and remedies. I have been quite unwell for a long time, and I consulted an Ngaka, who suggested I could become a healer, saying that it was a disposition that was in our family, as my grandfather had been an Ngaka. After a long period of trying to decide what to do, I came to a decision and for the first time in a very long time, I have started to feel better, and to be at peace.

LA: Do you connect the two in some way? Your need for healing, therapeutic writing, as you said and storytelling or writing?

PM: I'll have to see how that works itself out. I'm not very knowledgeable about this traditional healing, I never really followed it very closely. But of course I know many traditional healers. Beyond using herbs, they are also interested in stories. Because when people come to you and say, 'I've got a problem', you don't just say, 'Well is it a headache? Here is medicine for your headache', you also want to know how they are doing in their social relationships, because perhaps the headache might come from elsewhere, from a source other than a germ or virus. So you really have to be interested in stories, and I see a connection there. And of course if you hear stories and you see you have experiences of meeting people, then inevitably you'll also tell stories, whether that will translate into writing or not is something else. I hope in my case they'll translate into writing. I wouldn't mind writing a novel that shows someone that does traditional healing.

LA: So maybe it's a research opportunity as much as anything . . .

PM: [laughs]

LA: And it sounds like a form of psychoanalysis perhaps? The way you listen to stories and help to resolve things through other examples, it's very therapeutic.

PM: Ja, well I'm thinking along the lines of writing, not a book like that one, but it's just a book that comes to mind, a book by M. Scott Peck called *The Road Less Travelled.* I usually find books on psychotherapy, psychology and psychoanalysis extremely difficult to read, but I was always fascinated by the way he tells the stories of his patients, of course taking due care not to expose the patients. But he's got very fascinating stories that show a really fascinating link to storytelling and therapy.

LA: It's an argument for why narratives are so important. You impose a structure to make sense of your life, and everything that you experience, you tend to make a story. People make personal histories and family trees. It's all part of a process of trying to contain the world.

PM: And I actually think that in the novels that I've read in South Africa, we don't have much on traditional healing and I certainly see it as, I don't know if I'll be able to handle it, but I think I see it as an opportunity to contribute in that direction. So it's quite possible that my next project might be dealing with disease and storytelling.

LA: It's quite a mysterious area as well isn't it? It's a very secretive profession, the misperceptions of what happens would be worth revealing, from the inside . . .

PM: To the extent that it is possible and admissible [laughs]. Look, I mean, I must be clear, I think I also actually believe in the veil of secrecy. One has to be careful what one talks about and what one reveals. The whole idea behind freedom of expression – I value that as well, but I think there has to be a balance. Inevitably when you talk, you are going to offend some people, but I think there is something unethical about deliberately going out of one's way to offend.

LA: And do you think you would risk offence, by telling stories about this practice?

PM: No, but I think there will be certain elements which one may keep secret. Of course, I haven't been in that field yet myself. I wouldn't know the details of what might be made public, what may not be made public. But I think it happens everywhere. Even if you go to an everyday fulltime job, there are things you keep confidential, you know, [laughs] I think it's a basic thing on ethics and such things.

LA: Well good luck and thank you very much.

PM: It's a pleasure.

Johannesburg, 26 November 2004

Phaswane Mpe: Biographical Note

Phaswane Mpe was born on 10 September 1970 in what is now Limpopo Province. He attended St Bede's High School near Polokwane, matriculating in 1988, and went on to study at the University of the Witwatersrand in Johannesburg, where he completed his MA in African Literature in 1996. This was followed by a Diploma in Advanced Study in Publishing at Oxford Brookes University, Oxford, in 1997.

Between 1996 and 2001 Phaswane lectured in African Literature and Publishing Studies at Wits University, where he was held in high esteem by students and colleagues alike. Language and literature were his passion and he involved himself in every aspect of their promotion and exploration. He published numerous articles in local and international journals, contributed chapters to book anthologies, and submitted articles and book reviews for several newspapers. He also freelanced as an editor and reader for publishers. He was generous with his support for the creativity of others, actively encouraging the writing potential of his students and helping to set up the campus literary journal, *Jala*.

In 2001 his debut novel, *Welcome To Our Hillbrow* was published by the then University of Natal Press and went on to take the literary world by storm, both in South Africa and abroad. The novel received much acclaim and was shortlisted for several awards, including the Sanlam Literary Prize for Fiction in 2001 and the Sunday Times Fiction Award in 2002. It was included in the *Mail & Guardian*'s 101 books for Christmas (December 2001) and received a Meritorius mention in the NOMA Awards of 2001.

The pressure was on for Phaswane to produce a follow-up masterpiece, but his immersion in academics pulled him in competing directions. He received a sought-after doctoral fellowship from WISER – the Wits Institute for Social and Economic Research – and initially planned to do his PhD on issues around child rape and HIV/AIDS. He later changed his area of research to sexuality in post-apartheid literature.

In November 2004, battling increasingly bad health, Phaswane gave up his WISER fellowship and put his doctorate on hold in order to 'follow the call of his Ancestors' and train as a traditional healer, as his grandfather had done before him. He died unexpectedly on 12 December 2004 at the age of 34.

Glossary

1912 — The date that the South African Native National Congress was founded. (See SANNC.)

African Renaissance — A concept popularised by South African President Thabo Mbeki in the 1990s, which promotes African solutions to African problems, and the affirmation of African cultural values.

Afrikaans — The language of the Afrikaner people of South Africa, now spoken by a wide diversity of communities across the racial divide. Under National Party rule it was one of only two official South African languages. It was the attempt to enforce Afrikaans as the medium of instruction at black schools that sparked the Soweto uprising of 1976.

Agee ntate — Sepedi for 'I greet you, father'.

Aibo — Exclamation of surprise, dismay or pain.

Amabokoboko aya phumelela — Victory song sung by ecstatic rugby supporters to celebrate the winning of the Rugby World Cup by the South African Springbok Rugby Team in 1995; literally, 'The Boks have won'.

Amandla — Rallying cry of South African black people during the freedom struggle, especially at mass gatherings; literally, 'Power'.

ANC	African National Congress, formerly the leading liberation movement of the anti-apartheid freedom struggle and currently the ruling South African party.
Ancestors	Deceased elders, believed to be still living on in a spirit realm, who are venerated as a source of guidance, blessings and prosperity.
Bafana bafana	The South African national soccer team.
Bantu Education	An inferior system of education imposed on black South Africans during apartheid with the aim of keeping them pinned to their underclass status.
Barry Hertzog	A Boer War general and Prime Minister of the Union of South Africa from 1924 to 1939. He was dedicated to the preservation of the Afrikaner culture.
Benny McCarthy	Popular South African soccer player, now playing for international teams.
Bliksem	Afrikaans for 'beat up'; also used as an expletive, equivalent to 'damn it'. Its literal meaning is 'lightning'.
Blowing horn	The traditional means, in rural areas, of summoning the community to important gatherings; usually a kudu horn.
Boers	Afrikaans for 'farmers'; a collective term for Afrikaners, often used disparagingly.
Bone throwers	Diviners who make use of animal bones to access and interpret messages from the Ancestors.

Braaivleis	Literally, 'barbecue meat'; more generally used to refer to a barbecue.
Braamfontein	One of the older central suburbs of Johannesburg, where the University of the Witwatersrand is situated. It borders the inner city and is connected to the cultural node of Newtown by the landmark Nelson Mandela Bridge, constructed in 2003 as a symbol of planned inner-city rejuvenation.
Charles Mungoshi	Award-winning Zimbabwean author and poet, whose titles include *Waiting for the Rain* and *Coming of the Dry Season*.
Clement Doke	Well-known South African linguist who abandoned the customary Eurocentric approach to language in favour of one that recognised the very different grammatical structure of Bantu languages. He published several grammar works, dictionaries and a history of Bantu linguistics.
Comrades	A term of political solidarity widely used by activists during the South African freedom struggle and adopted by black youths as a general signal of brother- and sisterhood, especially during the 1970s and 80s.
Dagga	Marijuana.
Dompas	Literally, 'stupid pass'; the derisive term for the hated identity document that black South Africans were forced to carry. (See Pass Law.)
Donga	Eroded gully or ditch.
Dumpies	Small beer bottles that hold 340 ml.

East Rand	Commonly used term for the areas to the east of Johannesburg in the former Transvaal, now part of Gauteng.
Freedom Day	Commemorating the first democratic South African elections held on 27 April 1994, it is celebrated with a national public holiday.
Grens	Border.
Gumba	A popular term that signifies a rally or gathering; 'gumba gumba' is slang for a ghettoblaster music system.
Herbert Dhlomo (H.I.E.)	A respected figure in South African literature of the 1930s and 40s, and one of the first black writers to write prolifically in English. His long epic poem, 'Valley of a Thousand Hills', is one of his most acclaimed works.
Hector Peterson	One of the first casualties of police bullets during the 1976 Soweto student uprising. Only twelve years old, his tragic death was immortalised in a photograph by Sam Nzima and became an iconic image and rallying point of the struggle against apartheid.
Hillbrow	One of Johannesburg's most famous, and infamous, inner-city zones. Part urban slum, part cultural melting pot, it has one of the highest population density figures in the world and is well known for its violent crime, prostitution and destitution.
Houghton	Elite suburb in Johannesburg known for its liberal values and upper-class lifestyle.

Induna	Traditional headman or chief.
isiZulu	The language spoken by the amaZulu people of KwaZulu-Natal.
Izibongo	See Praise poem.
Ja	South African version of 'yes' (originally Afrikaans).
Khunwana massacre	Khunwana is a city in North West Province; the precise reference is, however, unknown.
Knobkerrie	A stick with a knobbed head, often used as a weapon.
Kraal	Fenced area of a homestead where cattle and other livestock are kept.
Kwaito	South African urban fusion music form that emerged in the 1990s, made popular by artists such as Mandoza, Zola, Bongo Maffin and others.
Lebowa	Formerly one of the 'homelands' or ethnically demarcated tribal areas in apartheid South Africa. Now incorporated into Limpopo Province.
***love*Life**	Slogan for a popular campaign that promotes safe sexual practices.
Madiba	One of Nelson Mandela's affectionate nicknames. Traditionally a respectful title given to elders of the clan, it has been adopted into widespread popular use.
Makwerekwere	Derogatory name given to foreigners, especially those from other parts of Africa.

Mary Metcalfe Committed anti-apartheid activist who played a prominent role in organisations such as Black Sash and Detainees' Parents' Support Committee (DPSC). She currently heads the Agriculture, Conservation, Environment and Land Affairs Policy Unit in Gauteng.

Matric Short for matriculation, the final school-leaving qualification, formerly known as Standard Ten (now Grade 12).

Mealie Corn on the cob.

Mfecane Refers to the period of widespread chaos and unrest in the early 1800s that coincided with Shaka's rise to military strength and campaigns of conquest against the Nguni tribes of the KwaZulu area. These led, among other things, to the formation of a unified Zulu nation.

Migrancy The condition of black job-seekers, forced to leave their homes and families in rural areas in order to seek work in urban centres and mines. Since they were usually able to return home only once or twice a year, and wives were not permitted to follow their men, it was not uncommon for migrants to construct a second family for themselves in the urban centre near which they were employed.

Necklace The gruesome method of killing by placing petrol-soaked tyres around the victim's neck and setting them alight. A tactic widely used by struggle Comrades in the 1980s and 90s against political opponents or those suspected of being 'sell-outs'.

Ngoako Ramatlhodi	The controversial former Premier of Limpopo, implicated in various corruption scandals.
Nkosi Johnson	South Africa's youngest AIDS 'ambassador', who won hearts all over the world with his heroic approach to his illness and his moving address, televised from the 13th International AIDS Conference in Durban in 2000. He and his foster mother Gail founded Nkosi's Havens, care centres for HIV/AIDS affected mothers and children. He died in June 2001 from AIDS-related complications.
Ntate	See Agee ntate.
Obet	Outcomes Based Education, also known as Obed. Controversial educational model adopted as a replacement for the old divisive, racially based South African syllabuses.
Oom Kruger	Refers to Paul Kruger, a prominent Boer resistance leader against British rule in the 1800s, who became President of the then Transvaal Republic.
Pass Law	One of the most tyrannical aspects of apartheid rule, this law required black people in urban areas to carry a 'pass' or identity document at all times and produce it on demand. Recorded on the pass were details of the person's ethnic group, job status and permission or otherwise to be in the specified area. Failure to produce the pass resulted in immediate jailing, a circumstance which made criminals of many thousands of black people during the apartheid years.

Peterson	See Hector Peterson.
Pietersburg	Now known as Polokwane, a large town near Pretoria in Limpopo Province.
Philippe Troussier	Former French rugby coach of the Springboks.
Population Registration Act	Mainstay of the apartheid separate development system, this required every South African to be classified according to the 'race group' to which he or she was deemed to belong, by virtue of skin colour, parentage and place of birth.
Praise poem	Traditional praise, sung or spoken, that conveys a person's origins, ancestors, achievements and other noteworthy life events.
Quartz Street	One of the more notorious Hillbrow streets, characterised by the aggressive prostitution of its 'pavement brothels'.
Quirinalle	A popular brothel on the border of Hillbrow and Braamfontein, reportedly since shut down.
Rainbowism	A reference to the unified 'Rainbow Nation' of 'new' democratic South Africa; a phrase first coined by Archbishop Desmond Tutu in the 1990s and widely adopted.
Richmond	A town in KwaZulu-Natal; one of the areas worst hit in the 1990s by the internecine violence between warring political parties in the run-up to the first South African democratic elections of 1994.

Rolihlahla	Nelson Mandela's isiXhosa name.
Sangoma	A traditional diviner.
SANNC	The South African Native National Congress. The forerunner of the African National Congress, it was founded in 1912 at a convention of prominent African intellectuals that included writer Sol Plaatje and educationalist John Dube, who was the first president.
Setswana	The language spoken by the Tswana people of North West Province and Botswana.
Sharpeville	Site of the infamous massacre of 21 March 1960, when police opened fire on a peaceful protest against the Pass Law.
Shosholoza	A popular South African 'working song', traditionally sung by manual workers to give rhythm to work by. Frequently sung at rugby matches by enthusiastic supporters of the Springbok Rugby Team.
Sibusiso Bengu	First post-apartheid South African Minister of Education.
Sol Plaatje	One of South Africa's most gifted black writers from the 1900s, held in high esteem for his literary excellence, outspokenness against oppression and tireless campaigning against discriminatory legislation. Author of *Mhudi*, the first novel written in English by a black South African, he also translated Shakespeare into Setswana.

Springboks	South Africa's national rugby squad, also known as 'the Boks' or 'Amabokoboko'.
Stimela	Popular South African music group of the 1980s and 90s, headed by Ray Phiri, which pioneered an innovative African Jazz fusion style. One of their hits was 'See the world through the eyes of a child'.
Super Eagles	Nigeria's national soccer team.
Trevor Manuel	South Africa's Minister of Finance from 1999 onwards.
Truth and Reconciliation Commission (TRC)	A nationwide platform set up in the mid-1990s to allow apartheid victims and perpetrators to come face to face, with the aim of exposing human rights abuses and uncovering the true fate of thousands of missing or murdered political activists. By this it was hoped to obtain the closure that would allow South Africans to move forward into a new era of post-conflict reconciliation.
Tsotsi	Gangster.
Tzaneen	Town in Limpopo Province.
Verwoerdian food for thought	Refers to Hendrik Verwoerd, Prime Minister of South Africa from 1958 to 1966, who instituted most of the major apartheid legislation that formalised racial separation and inscribed the inferior status of black South Africans.
Union Buildings	Located in Pretoria (Tshwane), site of the Administrative Capital of South Africa.

University of the North	Formerly known as Turfloop, one of the 'black' universities in segregated South Africa.
Urban Areas Act	Apartheid law forbidding black people to reside or work in so-called 'white' urban areas, unless by special permission.
Youth Day	A national holiday that falls on 16 June, in commemoration of the 1976 Soweto uprising, when protesting school children took to the streets and sparked a national revolution.